## A Candlelight Ecstasy Romance®

**"DON'T LET ME DIE, RYAN," KERI
BEGGED TEARFULLY.**

"You're not going to die, Keri," Ryan vowed
fiercely. "No one is going to take you away from
me. No one." He pressed a hungry kiss against her
temple and continued murmuring in her ear. The
words didn't always make sense, but they did comfort her.

"Don't leave me," Keri pleaded, grabbing hold
of his hand.

His smile was meant to reassure her and it did.
"Don't worry, I won't."

## CANDLELIGHT ECSTASY ROMANCES®

# GENTLE PROTECTOR

*Linda Randall Wisdom*

*A CANDLELIGHT ECSTASY ROMANCE*®

Published by
Dell Publishing Co., Inc.
1 Dag Hammarskjold Plaza
New York, New York 10017

Dell ® TM 681510, Dell Publishing Co., Inc.
Candlelight Ecstasy Romance©, 1,203,540, is a registered
trademark of Dell Publishing Co., Inc., New York, New York.

ISBN: 0-440-12831-5

Printed in the United States of America
First printing—March 1985

*For Evelyne and Beth. This is for all those telephone calls, our fits of laughter and times of moaning and groaning when something went wrong. Thanks for being there when I needed you.*

To Our Readers:

We have been delighted with your enthusiastic response to Candlelight Ecstasy Romances®, and we thank you for the interest you have shown in this exciting series.

In the upcoming months we will continue to present the distinctive sensuous love stories you have come to expect only from Ecstasy. We look forward to bringing you many more books from your favorite authors and also the very finest work from new authors of contemporary romantic fiction.

As always, we are striving to present the unique, absorbing love stories that you enjoy most—books that are more than ordinary romance. Your suggestions and comments are always welcome. Please write to us at the address below.

Sincerely,

The Editors
Candlelight Romances
1 Dag Hammarskjold Plaza
New York, New York 10017

# CHAPTER ONE

These business breakfasts were all alike and as boring as hell! Ryan grimaced as he entered the large banquet room filled with many white cloth-covered tables.

"You need to start attending these business functions," Jason Caldwell, his partner, had informed him the day before. "It's a great way to make contacts. You never know who you may meet."

"Sure—all the old-timers who think they were the ones to bring prosperity to the city," Ryan had answered.

Still, he showed up at the restaurant the next morning at seven sharp, was shown to the correct banquet room by an overly attentive hostess, signed in, and accepted the paper name badge; RYAN KINCAID, it said, with *Kin-Cal Property Investments* written underneath.

Ryan sauntered over to a long buffet table and poured himself a cup of coffee from the large urn. At least it was hot, if not totally drinkable. He turned to let his gaze wander over the room; standing apart from the group, he made an impressive image. Just over six feet, with hair the color of rich sable and eyes the same dark shade, he was an arresting figure in a dark blue three-piece suit with a pale blue shirt and matching tie. His lean body was that of a man who either didn't have to worry about his weight or worked diligently at keeping himself in shape. The dark tan attested to his love of the outdoors. A sprinkling of silver at the temples, and lines fanning out around his eyes, and faint lines around his mouth, indicated a man past the thirty-year mark and on his way to forty who'd be a remarkable-looking man even when he was sixty.

Ryan's eyes roamed over the clusters of people, passed over one group, then swung back again. He could only see her profile, but that was enough to capture his attention.

Hair the color of rich antique gold shone brightly under the artificial lights, and he'd wager his life that it wasn't the result of a hairdresser's careful coloring job. Cut just below chin length in a sassy style that feathered away from her face, it gave him an excellent opportunity to study her well-defined features. Even her smile in profile was enough to leave him stunned. He studied her left hand, which was holding a coffee cup. Her only ring was on the second finger and certainly didn't look like a wedding band or engagement ring. So far, so good.

As if she were aware that she was under observation, she slowly turned, allowing her eyes to sweep casually over the room until they encountered his dark eyes. For a moment they halted and widened slightly, as if sensing a message in their sable depths; then they swiftly looked away. He noticed with satisfaction that the hand that held the coffee cup wasn't quite as steady now.

Ryan took a quick swallow of his coffee, set the cup down, and looked around for Jason. When he found his partner, he quickly walked over to the other man.

"Ryan, glad to see you could make it." The gray-haired, portly man greeted him with a smile and clap on the shoulder. "I'd like you to meet—"

"First," Ryan interrupted him, "the woman over there in the far corner—dark-blond hair in a sort of blue dress: Do you know her?"

Jason glanced over in the direction Ryan indicated. "Keri Burke. She owns a temporary personnel agency."

"Introduce me."

The older man laughed as if he knew something Ryan didn't. "Old buddy, it would be easier for you to put the make on the queen of England than her."

"She's not married," Ryan stated flatly; yet, he was a little unsure of his statement.

"No, but she's dead set against men," Jason explained. "There have been those who have tried, but none have succeeded to my knowledge."

Ryan watched Keri, his brows knitted in a frown. "You can't mean she's—"

Jason laughed louder this time. "No, I just think she got burned badly and is a little gun-shy of men. Do yourself a favor and look around for someone else to play with," he advised.

Ryan merely smiled noncommittally and wandered off, keeping an eye on Keri Burke, positive that she was keeping a cautious eye on his prowling figure too. He was getting more curious about her by the minute. What color were her eyes? What was her preference in music? His instincts spoke loudly and clearly. She wasn't romantically involved . . . yet.

He deliberately stayed away from the group Keri was talking with, sure that if he approached her, she would find an excuse to leave. He'd bide his time until the moment was right. He didn't have to wait long.

When the time came for everyone to be seated, Ryan made sure he took a seat at Keri's table, directly across from her. When she flashed him a cool smile, he didn't smile in return and received a puzzled frown from her. Now he knew. Her eyes were a curious combination of blue and green, and in the cool depths there was just the slightest hint of sadness. Most people might not notice it, but he did because he had gone through a bad hurt himself. Was that why she steered away from men? He silently cursed the man who had hurt such a lovely woman.

Keri could feel a strange heat invade her body under Ryan's gaze. He was new to the area and to the club. She attended the monthly breakfasts on a regular basis and he hadn't been there before. She was sure of that. He was someone she definitely wouldn't have forgotten.

Of course, she had met Larry, an ex-boyfriend, there and she would never be able to forget the nightmare he had led her into. She was glad that he had left town, because she doubted that she would ever be able to face him again. Keri doubted that even the pain she had experienced due to her ex-husband Don's callous treatment of her could equal what Larry had done to her.

She picked up her glass of orange juice and let the chilled liquid slide down her suddenly parched throat.

Men had looked at Keri before, and she usually was able coolly to let them know she didn't appreciate them undressing her with their eyes. But this man was different. Oh, he was studying her with those dark eyes, but he wasn't mentally stripping her. He was much more dangerous because his thought processes were delving their way into her soul!

" 'K. Burke.' " His eyes swept over the badge stuck on the silky cotton just over her right breast. " 'K.B. Temps.' Are you related?"

Keri nodded. "I *am* K.B. Temps."

"Which is . . . ?" He arched a questioning eyebrow and leaned back in his chair, hooking an arm over the back. For a moment her eyes couldn't stray from the enticing sight of the front of his shirt stretched across his chest just above his buttoned vest.

She had a strong suspicion that he already knew about her agency but for some reason preferred to hear it from her. "I have a temporary personnel service." Her low voice was music to a man's ears.

"Clerical?" he quizzed.

"All phases, Mr. . . . ?" It was now her turn to study his name tag. ". . . Kincaid."

"How about a secretary familiar with real estate terminology, typing, shorthand, all the usual duties?" Ryan asked brusquely. "Someone who can take criticism without breaking down in tears, work overtime without complaining, and put up with a very bad-tempered boss?"

Keri's smile was more breathtaking when he saw it straight on. "Are you sure you haven't forgotten anything?"

"If she cracks under pressure just once, she'll be out on her can," he continued crisply, oblivious to the interested listeners at their table.

"Do I detect that you're giving me a job order?" She decided it would be better if she put this conversation on a businesslike basis right away. She thought that he would prefer to put it on another level altogether.

"As long as I don't get someone who looks as if she belongs in a centerfold," Ryan insisted.

Keri dug into her purse, pulled out her business card, and handed it across the table to Ryan. He returned the gesture with one of his own.

"The rate for such an impeccable character can be high," she cautioned lightly.

"As long as she's worth it," he told her in an arrogant voice.

Keri was grateful when scrambled eggs and bacon with hash brown potatoes and English muffins appeared. She already sensed that this very basic male was more than she cared to handle.

All the while she ate, she was very much aware of the man seated across from her. Ryan Kincaid was a go-getter. She could feel it in her bones that he was a man accustomed to getting his way, whether it concerned business or women. Right now he was busy exerting a potent charm over the other two women and two men at the table, especially the women. Even Addie Lake, a brusque, sharp-spoken woman in her fifties, had softened under Ryan's sincere interest in her gourmet shop.

Keri knew something the others didn't. Ryan had the uncanny ability to carry on a conversation with them while keeping his concentration solely on one person—her. The food was tasteless in her mouth. She wouldn't have a man in her life right now. She *couldn't* have one!

The speaker may have been good, but Keri didn't hear one word. She was too conscious of Ryan lounging in his chair, one hand resting on the snowy tablecloth.

What was it about him that attracted women? He didn't fit the conventional idea of a handsome man. His features were too rugged, his hands strong-looking, as if he enjoyed working with them; the fingers were slightly blunt at the tips, but she had a good idea that they could be gentle when stroking a woman. His jaw was uncompromising, his eyes too discerning. She felt as if he were seeking the path to her soul. He was a dangerous man

14

who would be more at home in the jungle than in civilization.

Keri suddenly felt very uneasy. She fumbled under the table for her purse and slipped out of her seat. She had never walked out during a speech before, but this year had been full of a great many firsts for her. As she crept out of the banquet room she sensed a pair of dark eyes burning into her every step of the way.

Serena, the receptionist at K.B. Temps, greeted her boss with a broad smile. Her silvery hair, kept in a neat coil on top of her head, and the lines fanning out from her eyes and cheeks proclaimed her to be in her late fifties or early sixties, but her energy and enthusiasm for her job belonged to a woman much younger.

"The breakfast is over so early?"

"No, I just wasn't interested in hearing about the benefits of advertising in local business magazines." She picked up the pink message slips marked with her name. "Are all our new lambs in safe and sound?"

Serena nodded. Part of her job was to call and verify that the workers had reported to their new jobs on the first day without mishap.

Keri walked back to her office, greeting the other two personnel consultants on the way. Mondays were always their busiest days, and this was no exception, judging by the constant ringing of the phones. The typewriter keys rattled in the background as an applicant took her typing test.

Keri closed her office door in order to have peace and quiet. She walked around her desk to her chair before sorting through her messages. The top one seemed to jump out at her: *Ryan Kincaid of Kin-Cal called. Please call him with the name of a replacement secretary.* According to the time jotted in the corner, the call hadn't been made more than five minutes after she had left.

She swiveled her chair around and switched on the small computer sitting on the credenza. In no time she had the pertinent information displayed on the screen. A number was punched out on the telephone and a seductive feminine voice answered the call: "Hello."

"Cassie, it's Keri." She settled the receiver firmly between her shoulder and jaw. "How would you like to begin work for a bad-tempered ogre tomorrow?"

Cassie's laugh was equally sensual. "Is combat pay involved?"

"I guarantee I'll make it worth your while, because you certainly deserve every penny. This man wants a virtual machine, and if anyone can make him toe the line, I'm sure you can," Keri said confidently.

"I take it he's good-looking."

"Cassie, your only duties are secretarial," she reminded with a laugh, acknowledging a private joke between the two women. "This man is a new client, and something deep down tells me that the agency could get a lot of business from him as long as he's happy with our service." Since Cassie had been one of Keri's first applicants and their working relationship had later grown into a close friendship, Keri knew she could talk to her bluntly. All she kept to herself was the fact that Ryan Kincaid was the kind of man to pack quite a punch in the masculinity department! That she preferred not to think about.

Cassie laughed. "All right, give me all the gory details. I'll keep him in line."

"Good enough. That's why I called you first." Keri

dug into her purse, drew out Ryan's business card, and read off his name, the name of the company, and the office address. "Give me a call at home tomorrow night and let me know how it looks over there. Just make sure you have him eating out of your hand—not taking a bite out of it!"

After Keri rang off with Cassie, she knew she had to make another call, which turned her hands to ice. It was a few moments before she could force her fingers to work properly. She was put through immediately.

"Kincaid." His throaty voice sent shivers along her spine.

"Keri Burke, Mr. Kincaid." The deep breath she had taken as she dialed kept her voice level. How could one brief meeting with this man affect her so? "I wanted to let you know that your temporary secretary is Cassandra Matthews." A tiny smile flitted across her lips when she quoted the rate.

"She'd better be worth every penny, Keri, or I'll take it out of your hide." There was no indication in his voice that he was surprised by the high rate.

Even the way he said her name made her nerve endings tingle. "I'm sure you'll be more than pleased with Cassie's performance." Her cool voice belied the tremors this man could create even across the phone. "I'll meet you for lunch tomorrow then and let you know what I think about your impeccable employee," Ryan inserted silkily.

Keri froze. He certainly didn't waste any time, did he? But then, Larry hadn't, either, when he first persuaded her to go out with him. "Isn't it difficult to evaluate a worker after only a few hours?" she said evasively.

"Honey, I'll know within five minutes if she'll work

17

out or not," he declared. "Since I'm fairly new to the area, I'll let you choose the restaurant."

"It's usually the agency who takes the client out," she protested stiffly.

"Fine with me. What time shall I pick you up?"

She had fallen very neatly into his trap! There was no way she could back out now. "I'll come by your office," she replied. "Is twelve-thirty all right?"

"No problem there. See you tomorrow, Keri. And the name is Ryan," he said, then hung up.

Keri set the phone down and leaned back in her chair. Even Larry hadn't affected her so potently in the beginning. The beginning . . . The end would be more like it.

She quickly wrote up the pertinent information and took the paperwork out to Serena. The receptionist glanced over the company name and arched an eyebrow.

"Hmm, Ryan Kincaid. He was the sexy voice this morning." She smiled up at her boss. "Where did you find him?"

"It was more like he found me," Keri explained dryly. "He was at the breakfast this morning."

"Talk about a fast worker," Serena teased, then softened at Keri's pale features. "You know very well you're not going to be able to hide out forever, Keri. We're all behind you here. If he tries anything, he'll have all of us going after him with clubs!" She laughed, hoping to brighten her boss's features.

It worked. Keri's smile was brief, but it was there. "I don't know what I would do if I didn't have all of you," she said, sighing.

"It would be so boring around here!" Barb, one of the consultants, walked up to Serena's desk and dropped a small stack of papers on it. "Mrs. Peterson called. She

18

wanted four accounts-receivable clerks first thing in the morning," she informed Keri. "Naturally she argued about the rate again."

"Naturally," Keri replied. "Was it the same old argument?"

"Of course. 'We've been clients of yours right from the beginning, Barbara dear. I don't understand why you can't make an exception in our case. After all, we have referred a great many businesses to your agency.' " Barbara mimicked the woman's nasal drawl perfectly.

"I bet she pinches the fruit in the supermarket too." Keri sighed, watching Serena turn to the small computer terminal at her desk and input the new information. The installation of the computers may have been expensive, but for finding data in a hurry, it was well worth the cost. Also, it had cut their file storage problems more than fifty percent.

"How about going out for Chinese food?" Barb suggested. "I've been having horrible cravings for chow mein over the weekend, but Craig hates Chinese food." Craig was Barbara's husband.

"Isn't it a little early?" Keri glanced over at the clock on Serena's desk and saw that it was just a little after twelve. Where had the morning gone? "I guess it isn't too early. Sure, why not? Vicky should be back around twelve-thirty and we can go then."

Keri returned to her office and decided to finish going over the billings for the previous week. Serena would be sending them out in the afternoon mail; Keri double-checked her figures before they were sealed in the envelopes. She went through the procedure not because she didn't trust the other woman but to keep herself up-to-date on the traffic in the office. She also did her fair share

19

of interviewing and testing applicants, especially when the office was busy. The business had grown a great deal in the past two years. Originally, she and Barb handled all of the client orders and the interviewing and testing of new applicants. But even now she would not withdraw from the working part of the agency. She had seen the owners of too many agencies drop out of the business end, only to appear when the money was available. The way her client load was increasing, she would have to think about hiring another consultant. She had already offered the position to Serena, but the older woman preferred to sit at the front desk, and Keri was grateful for that. Even on the busiest days the receptionist wasn't ruffled. She calmed down apprehensive applicants, listened to their problems, soothed angry clients before they were turned over to the consultants, and was always there when she was needed. No wonder her six grandchildren loved her so much!

Not long after twelve-thirty, Keri and Barb were seated in a small family-run Chinese restaurant.

"Now, tell Momma all about it," Barb instructed, once their orders had been taken and a pot of tea had been left at their table.

"What's this? Have you been taking lessons from Amanda?" Keri arched her eyebrows when she mentioned her sister.

The dark-haired woman grimaced. *"No one* could ever emulate the great Amanda!" Her eyes twinkled merrily.

"You're lucky. You've only known her a year; I had to grow up with her." Keri poured some of the fragrant golden tea into her cup. Individually her features could be considered ordinary, but together they presented the face of a woman men were attracted to. They always

20

noticed her lovely smile, but the pain and sometimes fear in her eyes was something they seemed to overlook.

"I understand that Cassie is going out to Kin-Cal Investments to work for one of the big men," Barb commented casually.

"That's right." She could match her tone for tone.

"I believe the name given was Ryan Kincaid."

Keri nodded. "I met him at the businessmen's breakfast this morning."

The brunette's eyes were filled with curiosity. "So that's why he's called us. He's more interested in our illustrious leader than our temp personnel," she observed smugly.

Keri shook her head. "I'm sure that if Mr. Kincaid has any kind of interest in me, he won't have it for long." She stopped when the waiter appeared with their food.

"I suppose I'll have to fight you for the sweet-and-sour shrimp," Barb drawled.

"To the death." Keri laughed.

Keri was glad when the work day ended and she could go home. Her condominium was situated in a large, sprawling complex bordered by a golf course. Because the price of each unit was determined by how close it was to the golf course or swimming pool, Keri's was comfortably situated in the middle.

Once inside she silently blessed the invention of air conditioning. She walked upstairs slowly and slipped off her business clothes, exchanging them for a pair of khaki shorts and a coral knit top. Then she ran back downstairs to the kitchen—a sunny room of blue and yellow—took a small casserole dish from the refrigerator, and slid it into the microwave. Five minutes later a hot meal was ready.

"Ah, the wonders of modern science," she said dramatically, pouring iced tea into a glass.

The small round glass-topped table outside on the small patio was set, complete with a blue-print quilted placemat and matching napkins. There she could relax and enjoy the sunset.

Keri enjoyed her way of life. She finally felt that she had control over her destiny—at least, a good part of it. Gone were her years of working for someone else and paying for her ex-husband, Don's, tuition, textbooks, and various school expenses, which hadn't been cheap. When he had worked his way into a partnership with a prestigious civil-engineering firm in Denver, he decided he didn't need a wife who could think independently. Fortunately, Keri had come out of the divorce with enough money to start her agency.

She had just loaded her dinner dishes in the dishwasher when the doorbell rang.

"Max!" she greeted the stocky man with a bright smile and a hug.

Max's gray eyes studied her intently. "You're too pale, lass." His speech was thick with a Scottish burr. "You don't get out enough."

"I get out more than enough," she replied with a smile.

"I thought we'd go for a walk."

Keri eyed the gruff man with warm affection. "Is this walk for me or for you?" she asked, a trace of suspicion in her voice.

"You know the doctor likes me to take a walk each day," Max rumbled, scratching his chin. His coarse features were slightly out of place from his many years as a well-known prizefighter in the British Isles. Upon realizing that his years in the ring were over, he had taken the money he had carefully saved over the years, moved to the United States, and settled in the warm and dry Arizona climate.

"Let me put on a pair of shoes." Keri hurried upstairs to pull on a pair of jogging shoes and drop her house key into the pocket of her shorts.

Max's heart condition required that he have some sort of moderate exercise, and most evenings Keri accompanied her kindly neighbor on his jaunt around the complex. Less than five minutes later they were walking briskly down the sidewalk.

"And how did you keep yourself out of mischief today?" she asked Max when they turned to cross a street.

"I played strip poker with two very lovely sixty-year-old ladies at the senior citizens' recreation center." He grinned wickedly.

"Ah!" Keri shrieked with laughter. "Talk about the original dirty old man!"

Max rubbed his fingers over a crooked nose that had been broken more than once. "Hell, woman, I may be an old codger in some people's eyes, but I'm far from the grave," he told her in his gravelly voice.

For some strange reason Keri could hear that remark come from Ryan Kincaid. Damn Kincaid for intruding on her thoughts!

Max glanced down in time to see an array of emotions crossing her face. "Are you feeling all right, lass?" he asked her gruffly.

"Just a little tired. It was a long day," she replied. They soon reached the more affluent condos facing the golf course. When they halted momentarily under a street lamp, they were unaware that they were being watched by a dark figure in a nearby upstairs window. He

23

stood there watching Keri take Max's arm and look up with a dazzling smile that hit the observer in the pit of his stomach. He drained the remaining Scotch in his glass and slowly turned away.

Tuesday was as busy as Monday. Keri pitched in wholeheartedly, interviewing new applicants and taking job orders from clients calling in.

Serena's voice crackled over the intercom. "Keri, Mr. Kincaid is on line three."

"Hopefully he's canceling lunch," she murmured, punching the appropriate button. "Good morning, Mr. Kincaid."

"What the hell is going on?" Ryan's roar assaulted her ears.

"I understand Cassie showed up on time," Keri said evenly.

"I specifically demanded no dumb broads, and what do you send me? Some blonde who looks as if she'd be happier in a bikini on the beach."

Keri sat back and tapped a pencil against the edge of her desk. She decided to wait for his tantrum to run out. Longtime experience told her that keeping a cool head in this type of situation was her best bet.

"Well?" he demanded an answer.

"Cassie has been employed as the administrative assistant to the chairman of the board of Computer Business Technology for eight years. Before that, she worked in the executive secretarial capacity for two other directors within the same company," Keri reeled off crisply. "She types 110 words per minute, takes shorthand at 120, and has glowing recommendation letters from her former employers. She also worked for a real estate broker's firm

24

before she came to me. That woman has more business sense in her little finger than many executives have after many years in their respective fields."

"If she's such a paragon, why would she want to work as a temp?" he asked.

"She doesn't care to work for just one person on a permanent basis when she can have a wide variety in the jobs the agency sends her on," Keri answered smoothly. She couldn't begin to count the number of clients who had wanted to hire Cassie on a permanent basis, but the blond woman had always turned them down. "Have you found fault with Cassie's work so far?"

"None, and you knew I wouldn't." She could have sworn there was a smile behind the words. "I'll see you at twelve-thirty, then. Do me a favor and choose someplace quiet for lunch. I'm not into fast-food restaurants."

Keri hung up and shook her head in amazement. Ryan was a total chameleon with regard to moods. At first she would have sworn he was going to snap her head off; instead he reverted to charm to remind her about lunch.

Kin-Cal Investments was housed in a well-spaced-out one-story building. Keri studied the directory and headed in the proper direction.

She could claim all she wanted that she wasn't looking forward to this luncheon engagement, but still, she had chosen an apricot silk blouse, a natural-colored linen skirt with a back slit for comfortable walking, and a matching linen jacket. Tan suede open-toed pumps flattered her slender legs, and the high, ruffled collar on her blouse added a touch of femininity to the otherwise severe outfit.

The office suite was decorated in soothing earth tones

25

with a plush rust-colored carpet underfoot. The red-haired receptionist matched so well that she looked like part of the decor.

"May I help you?" Her voice even had the proper relaxing tones.

"Keri Burke to see Mr. Kincaid," Keri said crisply.

The receptionist punched out a number and spoke into the telephone receiver. "Ms. Burke is here to see Mr. Kincaid." When she finished, she glanced up. "Mr. Kincaid's secretary will be out in a moment," Keri was duly informed.

Keri flashed her a brief smile and wandered over to a nearby easy chair. A few moments later Cassie walked out.

"Hello, Keri!" she greeted her friend warmly. "Ryan would like you to come back for a moment." She lowered her voice as they walked down the hall. "Your ogre was not too happy this morning."

Smiling, Keri turned to Cassie. The woman was tall and slender, with silvery-blond curly hair falling loosely to her shoulders. Her face belonged more to a model than a hardworking secretary with a husband and two small boys. At the age of thirty-eight she looked ten years younger. "He didn't think someone could look the way you do and be able to type with more than two fingers."

Cassie shot her a sly glance. "Isn't it surprising that his voice takes on a different tone when he speaks of you?" she mused.

Keri replied with a stony look. "You, of all people, should know better," she muttered fiercely.

Cassie grimaced. "Larry deserves to be shot—right after we do away with Don," she decided, once again going over a well-known subject between the two women. She

26

passed her desk and paused to rap her knuckles on a carved door nearby. After hearing a muffled reply, she opened it. "Ms. Burke is here, Ryan," she announced, practically pushing Keri inside.

Ryan was dressed more casually today, wearing a pair of navy slacks and a white knit polo shirt that focused the viewer's attention on the strongly carved tanned features.

"Very prompt." He cast approving eyes over her slim figure, liking what he saw.

Feeling uneasy under his assessing gaze, Keri spun around and studied the office interior. A large city map occupied one wall; beneath it was a drafting table covered with blueprints and architect's drawings. A dark-blue sofa sat against one wall with an oil painting of a desert scene hanging over it.

Ryan's desk held a great many sheets of paper, but his clutter had an orderly air about it: It was well organized in its own way, everything pretty much in its place, just like the man himself.

"I'll give you a tour after lunch." Ryan smiled, crossing the room toward her. "Right now, food is of major importance. I skipped breakfast." His hand would have cupped her elbow, but she neatly evaded his touch by stepping away. Undaunted, he walked close enough that she could smell a hint of fresh after-shave and the clean scent of male skin—a dangerous combination.

"We'll be back in about an hour and a half, Cassie," he said as they walked past her desk.

Keri barely remembered being propelled out the offices and into the warm sunshine as they walked toward the parking lot.

"If you'd like, I'll drive," Ryan offered, finally breaking the silence.

"Don't you trust women drivers?" A touch of mischief curved her lips.

He turned his head to look down at her. *"You* I'd trust with my soul," he murmured.

Keri could feel her body temperature rise. "Then you'd better drive," she told him in a cool voice.

He merely smiled and gestured toward a gunmetal-colored Porsche. He made no further attempt to touch her when they reached the sports car. In no time Keri was comfortably ensconced in the leather bucket seat.

"I'll need directions," Ryan said, sliding into the driver's seat.

Keri mentioned a nearby restaurant that featured old-fashioned country cooking. Following her instructions, they arrived there in less than ten minutes.

"Hmm, I didn't know about this place." Ryan got out of the car and went around to open Keri's door.

The exterior represented a ranch-style bunkhouse, complete with a hitching post in front.

"It's off the beaten track for tourists, so you don't get too large a crowd during the lunch hour," Keri explained as they walked up to the saloon-style swinging doors.

Inside, the walls were covered with replicas of wanted posters, handguns, and rifles, along with various branding irons. A young woman in a pink gingham dress and frilly white apron flashed a bright smile at Ryan and led them to a corner table.

"What do you recommend?" he asked Keri when they opened the menus.

"I like their chicken and dumplings," she replied.

"Sounds fine with me, as long as I can have apple pie for dessert."

After giving their order to the waitress, Ryan turned back to Keri.

"Does *Ms.* stand for Miss or ex-Missus?" he asked curiously.

"Ex-Missus," she replied curtly, concentrating her attention on her glass of water.

"How long?"

"A little over two years. Weren't we coming here to discuss business?"

"Does he still live around here?" Ryan persisted, ignoring her subtle plea to drop it.

Keri's jaw tightened. "His name is Don Patterson. I took back my maiden name after the divorce. He's a partner in a civil-engineering firm in Denver, where I used to live. A wife who could hold down a good-paying job was fine while he was in school, but after he began making his way in the world, he decided he wanted a decoration in his home instead. I moved to Tucson right after we separated three years ago and worked for an agency a friend of mine ran until I gained enough contacts to open my own office," she explained.

"Obviously it wasn't a friendly divorce," Ryan commented, placing his clasped hands on the table in front of him.

Her lips curled in a mirthless smile. "It was—until I demanded my share of the community property. Even though I made the house and car payments, I wasn't expected to receive any of the proceeds from the marriage."

Keri was glad when their meal arrived. She was afraid to have Ryan probe into her life too deeply just now.

Luckily he steered the conversation to questions about Keri's agency and volunteered information about his own work. The time passed pleasantly until it was time to leave.

As he had promised, Ryan took Keri on a tour of his office. She ignored Cassie's saucy wink when they passed her desk.

Afterwards he walked her out to her Sirocco.

"Now that we have business out of the way, how about dinner Friday evening?" He placed an arm on the car roof and leaned over slightly to look at Keri, who was now seated inside her car.

"I don't think so," she replied without hesitation.

"Is there someone in your life, Keri?" One of his fingers explored the line of her jaw until she moved her head away from his tantalizing touch.

She shook her head. "I do fine on my own," she said tersely.

"Have a heart, honey," Ryan implored. "I'm new in town, and while I'd like to try some of the nightspots, I hate to eat alone. No strings attached. Honest."

A brief smile tugged the corners of Keri's mouth. He wasn't an easy man to turn down. "On one condition."

"Which is?"

"You stop calling me honey." She switched on the engine.

"Seven o'clock?"

"All right." She gave him her address. Too bad she had to make sure this would be the only time she'd see him on a social basis, but it was all for the best.

"Dress very casual," Ryan advised her before he straightened up and moved away from the car.

When Keri drove away, she was already wondering what she was getting herself into. Ryan Kincaid spelled *danger* in her emotional life.

# CHAPTER TWO

After she returned to her office, Keri evaded many of the curious questions that came her way concerning her lunch with Ryan.

"Did he ask you out again?" Serena asked bluntly, following Keri into her office. The older woman had taken her boss under her wing, and was determined to help Keri find the loving man she deserved in her life.

"I am not dating the man." Keri sifted through her telephone messages, halted at one, and looked up at the receptionist with a sigh of impatience. "Don't tell me: Sheila doesn't like *this* assignment either?"

Serena nodded. "Helen talked to her for quite a while, but she still wanted to hear from you."

Keri exhaled wearily. She flopped into her chair and wondered if she shouldn't have become a circus clown. It had seemed a good idea when she was five years old. "She may not like it after I finish with her. She's done nothing but complain about the last three assignments, and the reports on her work performance have been less than favorable. I don't need anyone like her to give the agency a bad name." She finished glancing through her messages.

"Would you like some coffee?" Serena asked as she turned to leave.

Keri took off her jacket and draped it over the back of her chair. "If you wouldn't mind, I'd prefer a cup of tea."

"Tea coming up."

After Keri had a short talk with Helen, she made her call to the disgruntled temporary employee. Sheila had become a complainer lately. Keri was determined to find out if she had a legitimate reason for her actions. If not, she wouldn't be reassigned. K.B. Temps was known for its efficient employees. If the client didn't receive his money's worth, he would not use the agency again or refer new clients to it.

While Keri worked that afternoon, brief thoughts of Ryan flitted through her mind. Her body tightened in response. She had never met a more vitally alive man. She smiled to herself, thinking back on parts of their conversation at lunch. It hadn't been all that long, but she had already forgotten what it was like to have a handsome man pay attention to her.

No, not handsome. Good-looking, very masculine, a man fashioned to complement a woman's femininity and sensuality. She winced at the thought of that last word. She wanted nothing to do with emotions now. Once was more than enough.

The rest of the week went by at a smoother pace.

In the evenings Keri walked with Max, enjoying his reminiscences about his boxing days in Scotland. His many years gave him an abundance of stories.

"What would you say to taking in a movie tomorrow evening?" Max suggested when they went for their walk Thursday evening.

"I can't, Max," she answered with genuine regret. "I'm . . . ah . . . I'm seeing a client." She wasn't exactly lying.

The crusty old man scowled, not truly believing her glib reply. "A man?" His fondness for her had given him a paternal attitude toward her.

"A client, Max," she reminded him gently.

He scratched his head in thought. "So was the other," he replied gruffly. "I won't have another man hurt you, lass."

Keri felt a rush of affection. She hugged him tightly, ignoring his embarrassed protests. "Watch it, girl, I'm old enough to be your grandfather," he mumbled, his grizzled features growing redder by the minute.

"Don't worry, Max," she assured him lovingly. "This time I'd merely hand him over to you."

"You just be careful," he cautioned her. "Men today don't treat a lady like yourself the way she should be treated."

Keri privately thought that Ryan would treat a woman with the utmost courtesy, but something else nagged at her. He was also a man who would expect more from a woman. And that was something she wasn't prepared to give—to anyone.

When Keri arrived at the office on Friday morning, she had every intention of canceling her date with Ryan. She even went so far as to pick up the phone and call his office. First she chatted with Cassie, who had already told her that Ryan was a courteous, thoughtful boss. He might raise his voice and appear to breathe fire occasionally, but only when necessary. Before she could lose her nerve, Keri finally asked to speak to Ryan, only to be told that he was out looking at some property. Cassie promised to have Ryan return her call as soon as he returned to his office.

It didn't help that Friday was one of the agency's slow days, which gave Keri more time to mull over her error in allowing Ryan to maneuver her into going out with him.

The lunch hour came and went without a phone call from Ryan. Keri gritted her teeth and called his office again.

"You mean he hasn't called you yet?" Cassie was clearly surprised when Keri asked if Ryan had returned. "He came in about eleven. Let me buzz him."

Keri sat back while the silence on the phone assaulted her ear.

Cassie came back on the line. "Keri? He asked if he could call you back."

"I'd appreciate it," she replied coolly, then berated herself for taking her displeasure out on the wrong person.

Ryan didn't call until forty minutes later. An aggrieved Keri purposely kept him on hold a few moments before picking up the phone.

He cut in before she barely got her name out. "I won't let you do it, Keri." His voice flowed over her like rough velvet.

"Do what?" she asked, suspicious at having been put on the defensive.

"Back out of our date." Ryan was clearly the aggressor.

"It's not a date," she protested feebly. "I don't believe in mixing business and social contacts."

"Then I'll just have to find another agency, won't I?" He was now betraying his ruthless side. "Because I fully intend for us to get to know each other much better."

Keri could feel her stomach muscles tightening under

Ryan's caressing voice. Even over the telephone line he could weave his magic spell.

"I'll see you at seven, Keri." Ryan thought her silence meant further hesitation. "Don't forget to dress casual." With that, he hung up.

Keri put down the receiver and stared at her desk. "He wants casual, I'll give him casual."

That evening she dressed in a pair of comfortable old jeans that molded to her curves with loving detail. She topped them with a lightweight teal-blue V-neck pullover sweater with a plain Oxford shirt underneath. Tennis shoes completed her outfit.

When the doorbell rang, Keri could feel the butterflies in her stomach. She passed her tongue over dry lips and pulled open the front door. Her eyes widened when she saw Ryan dressed as informally as she was.

"Perfect," he pronounced, entering without waiting for an invitation. "You ready? I've got reservations for seven-thirty."

"I take it we're not going to that new French restaurant that just opened off Palmer," she said dryly.

Ryan grinned, looking ten years younger. "Nope, I've got that saved for tomorrow night." He reached out for her hand, but when she drew back, he only smiled and gestured to the door. "Shall we go?"

"What makes you think that I'll go out with you tomorrow night?" Keri asked caustically.

"Easy. You'll probably be so mad over tonight, you'll be eager to go out to an expensive restaurant and eat your way through my bankbook."

Keri studied his face. There was a tense, watchful quality in the dark eyes. There was more to his plans for the evening than he was telling her, and it had nothing to do with sex. That she was sure of, because if it had, she would have immediately shown him the door.

"I'm ready," she informed him, walking over to a nearby chair to pick up her shoulder bag.

Ryan walked over to the archway leading into the living room. He looked around at the pale cream couch, two gold easy chairs, and the celery-green plush carpet. A large painting of a desert scene executed by a local artist hung on one wall. A small light shined in a glass-doored cabinet on the opposite wall. He wandered over to get a better look at the contents.

He turned his head and smiled. "You don't look like the type to have an interest in fantasy art." He tipped his head toward her special menagerie.

Keri followed his gaze with a soft smile. What had he noticed first, the blown-glass griffin or the polished pewter sorcerer with his special wand? Perhaps the dark green dragon with its waving tail. There was even a translucent china Pegasus with his wings spread for flight, and a small gray castle with tiny yellow slits for windows.

"What, no princess?" he murmured, studying the many figurines, including a fine china unicorn with a circlet of flowers around its neck. "Or Prince Charming?"

"They're a part of fairy tales." She shrugged his question off.

Ryan looked down at her, sensing her withdrawal and seeing yet another side of her character. Just how many compartments were there that made up her personality? No matter: He would eventually discover them all.

"Ready?" His smile warmed his austere features.

Keri felt herself drawn more and more to Ryan. What helped was that he hadn't come on strong to her. Oh, he had practically bullied her into going out with him tonight, but deep down she knew that if she had been more adamant in her refusal, he would have accepted it.

"I haven't bowled since high school," she warned him after he had informed her of their destination.

"Good, I won't feel so bad when I beat the pants off you." He grabbed her hand and pulled her out of the house after reminding her to make sure that the front door was securely locked after them.

Keri felt herself transported back to her high school dating days when she and Ryan entered the noisy bowling alley.

"What size shoe do you wear?" he asked her when he was checking in at the desk.

"Five."

Ryan took the two pairs of shoes and score sheet and turned to Keri. "We're on lane eighteen," he told her, leading the way.

When they sat down on the bench to put on their bowling shoes, Keri looked around with interest. For a few moments she watched one curvy brunette who was wearing a red silky jumpsuit that would have been more appropriately worn on a disco dance floor than in a bowling alley.

"Hey, quit checking out the guys," Ryan teased. "You'll give me a complex."

Keri shook her head. "You'd be the last person to suffer from a complex. I was just wondering how she could bowl in something so tight," she said, motioning in the direction of the brunette.

Ryan barely gave the woman a cursory glance. "If she splits a seam, there's going to be a stampede in that direction. Come on, let's get our bowling balls."

After a few practice rolls Keri found the skill coming

back to her. Ryan observed her rolls and made helpful suggestions during their first game.

During one roll, which turned out to be a strike, Keri jumped up and turned around to find Ryan watching her intently.

"Now I know why I wanted to bring you bowling," he said, his dark chocolate eyes dancing with laughter.

She put her hands on her hips and glared at him, but it was hard to stay angry at a man who had just paid her a compliment. A few minutes later, while watching Ryan bowl, Keri had to admit that he was right. The view was certainly fascinating! His faded jeans fit his body like a second skin, as did his dark emerald sweater. He exuded an electric magnetism that was hard to ignore. She was beginning to see how much of a mistake it had been to go out with him tonight.

"I don't see how you can stand that vile-tasting stuff." Keri wrinkled up her nose when Ryan offered her some of his beer. She refused, preferring to stick with her soda.

"It's the only thing to drink with pizza," he replied as he offered her another dripping cheese slice covered with chopped mushrooms.

Keri leaned back against the low wooden bench that lined the wall. She would have never expected to spend an evening at a bowling alley and a pizza parlor with a man as sophisticated as Ryan Kincaid!

She saw Ryan as a man happier in an elegant French restaurant or spending his weekends playing golf or tennis. A majority of the men she knew who had risen as far as he had in the business world wanted to forget the more plebeian tastes that they had enjoyed in high school and college, having discovered much more refined pastimes.

Could she have misjudged him altogether? She wasn't sure if she truly wanted to find out.

Yet, Ryan seemed so at ease here, chatting amiably with the young man at the order window, who was a college junior, and the girl who had taken their drink orders. Larry wouldn't have been caught dead in a place like this.

"The last time I was in a pizza parlor with a member of the opposite sex, I was seventeen," Keri mused, watching the kids avidly playing the video games lining one wall.

"Didn't your ex-husband like pizza?" Ryan turned to face her, propping his elbow on the back of the bench, his cheek resting against his knuckles.

Keri couldn't help but notice how his fingertips brushed against his lips. For one wild moment she wondered what they would taste like. She mentally berated herself. That was the last thing she should think about!

"He . . . ah . . . he didn't like to go out. At least, not with me," she replied with a weak smile.

"Is he the reason you're uneasy around men?" Ryan's fingers reached out to smooth a stray strand of her hair, and he couldn't help but notice how she pulled her head so stiffly away from his touch. He frowned. When he had taken hold of her hand earlier that evening, she hadn't withdrawn. Now, when his touch became more personal, she closed up, the way the leaves of a mimosa would curl up for self-protection when something touched them.

"I don't like people probing into my life." Keri's voice was cool, even though she wanted to turn her face and rub her cheek against his knuckles. With Larry she had never felt this immediate physical attraction. She had to

39

stop it—now! This was dangerous. It could only lead to pain, and she had had enough of that lately.

"Don't shut me out, Keri," Ryan pleaded softly, noticing her emotional withdrawal. "Let me know the real you. Not the one you show to the world at the chamber-of-commerce breakfasts and to your clients. I want to find out about the woman hiding deep inside."

The one thing he hadn't expected was her bitter smile. "No, I don't think you'd want to know the real me, Ryan." The taut expression on her face suggested that he not probe any further into her comment.

He instinctively knew it was time to back off from questioning. "Tell you what: I'll be a gentleman and offer you the last piece of pizza," he told her. "But I know how you women are so calorie-conscious, so I'll just take temptation out of your way." He began to reach toward the pan.

"Wrong," Keri corrected smoothly, inwardly relieved that he had chosen to change the subject. She didn't think she could rehash the past just yet. "Pizza has always been my downfall, and there are times when I find it hard to believe that you're a gentleman." She plucked the pizza neatly out of his hand and bit into it.

"Then the least you can do is share," he grumbled, circling her wrist with his fingers and guiding the pizza toward his open mouth. Keeping his eyes trained on her flushed features, he bit through the cheese and dough, chewing slowly. "I think I like it better this way." He then directed her hand back to her mouth for a bite.

Keri knew she couldn't finish it now. "If you had wanted it so badly, all you had to do was say so," she informed him, offering him the rest of the slice.

Ryan's smile was a little too unnerving, as if he could read her tumultuous thoughts.

Keri was relieved when they got up to leave ten minutes later. Ryan drove smoothly and parked the car in front of her house, getting out to assist her.

Her stomach contracted painfully as she walked slowly up the short walkway to her front door with Ryan just a step behind her. Could she handle a quick good night and duck inside without looking like a fool? Oh, why had she let him bully her into going out with him tonight?

"Thank you. I really had fun," she murmured politely but sincerely, spinning around to face him as they reached the door.

"Does this mean you won't break the bank at dinner tomorrow night?" A faint smile curved his lips as he looked down at her uplifted face.

"I already have plans for tomorrow night," she lied, fully aware that he didn't believe her. "It looks like you're let off the hook," she said brightly, wishing to break his unnerving stare.

"Then the least you could do is invite me in for coffee," Ryan coaxed, sliding his hand over her shoulder and feeling the muscles tense under his touch.

"It's late," Keri protested lamely, moving away to evade any further caress.

One dark eyebrow arched in mocking question. "Ten-thirty is late?" he taunted.

"For me it is." She tipped her head back farther and almost gasped at the silvery moonlight casting dangerous shadows over Ryan's face.

"Then if you feel it's late, I could always come in to help you turn down your bed."

She almost let loose a burst of desperate laughter at his

41

obvious suggestion. As long as he kept it light and teasing, she was safe. "I don't think so."

"Choose which nightgown you'll wear?" he asked hopefully.

She shook her head.

"You don't wear a nightgown?" Ryan asked with an optimistic air.

"No, I don't need your help in choosing one." She laughed softly. She had forgotten how much fun outrageous banter could be, but it ended all too soon.

"You're a lovely woman, Keri, but you know that, don't you?"

"I know enough to fear a man's compliments." Her caution immediately communicated itself to him.

Ryan frowned. "You don't have to fear me, Keri," he said quietly, moving closer to her.

She swallowed, afraid of screaming out the frightened words filling her brain. "Please, Ryan," she pleaded, wetting her dry lips with her tongue. "Don't."

His eyes fastened on the provocative action. He looked as if he had already tasted her mouth and now wanted more. "Just a good-night kiss, Keri," he whispered, smoothing his hands over her shoulders and drawing her stiff body to him. "Is that too much to ask?" One hand slid up under her soft hair and curled around her nape. The massaging action was enough to turn any woman's bones to jelly.

*Yes!* Her mind screamed as her widened eyes watched his head tip slightly to one side and slowly lower, until his lips were a breath away from hers . . . then upon them in a feathery caress.

There was no demanding for surrender in his soft kiss, not even as the tip of his tongue outlined her lips and slid

42

over the smooth surface of her teeth, silently asking for a soul-shattering entrance, which she denied. Her body quivered, and she felt a raging fire burn through her veins. A kiss as soft as this had never affected her so potently before. Keri had a strong sensual nature, although no man had ever been able to tap into it as quickly and easily as Ryan was just doing. If anything, he had only discovered the tip of the iceberg.

"Relax, honey," he murmured against her lips, drawing her more closely toward his chest.

Keri shook her head violently. She wished her hands would obey the dictates of her brain and push him away instead of tunneling under the hem of his sweater to encircle his bare waist. His skin was so warm! She could feel the heat of his body reaching out to her and knew that if this kept up, it could only end one way, and she wasn't ready for that. There were too many factors to take into consideration. She had to think rationally. She just had to!

Ryan's hold tightened while his soft words urged her to melt against him. His hands roamed in a caressing fashion over her back and down to the rounded curves of her hips and buttocks. He wondered how long it had been since a man had held and caressed her this way. He could feel the tension in her body and kept his riotous response in check. She had been a married woman; yet, now she was as skittish as a virgin. Why?

Keri could feel her body begin to respond at the same time her mind rebelled. There was no threat in Ryan's embrace, only a warm comfort, but it could turn out to be a dangerous kind of solace. The soft moan in the depths of her throat was barely audible, but Ryan heard it and understood its meaning. His lips teased the outer

43

curve of her ear as they moved down to her earlobe. His teeth found the shape and taste of the shell-pink semicircle intriguing. When finished there, he nibbled his way along the fragile line of her jaw. Her soft sighs told him more of how he was affecting her than any words could. It was more than enough to excite him. One of his hands rested just below the curve of her breast, not too close but close enough for her sensitive skin to feel. Each time he moved his hand toward her taut nipple, she would stiffen. His lips would then turn soft and coaxing, and his hand would return to its original place. He didn't know why, but he was taking more time with her than he had with any other woman. There was something so vulnerable about her, as if she needed a man's loving tenderness instead of his passion. Deep inside he felt she would respond to the latter with an equal unbridled response of her own, but he knew it wasn't the time to find out, even though she felt so right in his arms! She fitted so perfectly against his body. No woman had curved naturally against him the way she did. She was not someone to be rushed but to be wooed and savored the way a fine wine should be appreciated. The end result would be well worth the effort. He pulled her more tightly against himself and thrust his hips enticingly against her body. She was pinned gently but securely between the front door and Ryan's body.

"Oh, Keri," he whispered, moving in closer against her. "I want to make love to you. Let me."

His words, spoken in his husky voice, and the feel of his potent arousal against her stomach was enough to shake Keri out of her trance. A garbled sound of fear tore from her throat as she jerked away from Ryan's arms.

"What am I doing?" she moaned. She looked up at

him with pain-filled eyes. "This is insane, Ryan. It can't happen again."

"Why not?" he demanded in a puzzled voice, moving forward to take her into his arms again, but stopped as she backed away from him. He didn't want to believe that the look of alarm on her face was real. "What kind of game are you playing here, Keri? Is your little frightened act just that—an act? Do you like to get a man all tied up in knots, then push him away? Don't you know what that does to a man?" His lips curled into a grim sneer.

Keri's eyes filled with tears. "I'm not that way at all." She gulped, then plunged ahead. She had nothing to lose now. "I find you very attractive, Ryan, but right now I can't have any further complications in my life."

Ryan smiled wryly at her words. "I've never been described as a complication before. Well, I guess if we have to start somewhere, it may as well be with me as your new problem. I don't intend to walk away from you now, Keri." His quiet voice held more than he cared to reveal just yet.

"I think it would be better if we didn't see each other again on a social basis," she announced, nervously twisting her shoulder bag strap. "Not when we have to deal with each other on a professional level also. That type of relationship never works out." How well she knew that!

"And I think it better that we do," Ryan responded, bracing one hand against the door so that she couldn't get away as easily the next time.

Keri shook her head violently. "You don't understand!" she cried out, fumbling inside her bag for her door key and half turning to insert it in the lock. Once she had pushed it open, she turned back to him. "The reason I don't want to see you again on a social basis is because I'm ten weeks pregnant," she blurted out, without any emotion portrayed on her delicate features. It took all of her courage to tell him this, and it was taking a great deal more to look up into his eyes. She wasn't surprised by what she saw there. "Good night, Ryan." She slipped inside and quietly shut the door.

Ryan stood stock-still as her announcement sunk in. His face was gray from the shock he had just received. He turned and walked slowly back to his car. He opened the door, then remained standing there for a moment staring at the building before him.

"Damn!" His palm hit the car roof with a resounding thud, but the physical action didn't help. The only pain he felt was the burning in his gut. For that moment, as far as he was concerned, the entire world was confined to hell.

Keri stood just inside the door, leaning back against the panels. Her eyes burned with unshed tears. The sound of squealing tires as Ryan drove off tore through her nerves.

"Oh, Ryan," she whispered into the silent air. "I'm so sorry." She straightened up and slowly climbed the stairs, taking one step at a time—the same way she was trying to live her new life, which had no room in it for a man like Ryan Kincaid.

# CHAPTER THREE

Unable to sleep more than a half hour at a time without nightmares of Ryan's shocked face haunting her, Keri finally abandoned her bed. She wandered downstairs to her kitchen and filled a ceramic teakettle with water. Later she carried a cup of cinnamon-and-spice herbal tea and two slices of toast to the kitchen table. Even that was tasteless this morning.

Keri still wasn't able to get the image of Ryan's stunned reaction out of her mind. She doubted she ever would be able to.

*I can imagine he's never had a woman tell him that she's pregnant when they're only on their first date,* she thought, deciding that the only way she could handle it was to find some kind of humor in the situation, however little it might be.

After breakfast Keri dusted the furniture, vacuumed the carpeting, and made her bed. Then, unable to resist the lure of the warm morning sunshine, she dressed in a pair of white cotton walking shorts, a mint-green T-shirt, and jogging shoes. She brushed her hair up in a short, bouncy ponytail.

Since Max had gone fishing with a few of his poker buddies that weekend, Keri's walk would be a lonely one. She wasn't sure if she wanted company that morning anyway. She knew that if Max were with her, he would invariably ask about her evening out, and she doubted she would be able to tell him the whole story.

Keri decided to walk down to the edge of the golf course to watch the Saturday-morning golfers. She found a small grassy knoll that would be safe from any stray balls shot by some of the more enthusiastic and less skillful sportsmen.

It soon turned out to be a mistake to sit there. The morning breeze caressed her cheeks with the same lazy warmth that Ryan's hands had bestowed on her the night before. The soft chattering of the birds brought back the memory of his murmurings in her ear. Her stomach tightened as her thoughts grew wider in scope. Goose bumps danced along the surface of her skin even though the sun was warm. Funny, no man had intruded his way into her mental wanderings since . . . She shook her head to free her mind. This wasn't the time to dwell on that.

Sighing wearily, she rose to her feet and dusted off the backside of her shorts. Perhaps if she went home and cleaned the two bathrooms, she'd feel better. If nothing else, it would tire her out enough to take a nap in the afternoon and catch up on her lost sleep from the previous night.

As she walked home along a narrow cement path that cut across the lawn on the edge of the course, Keri mentally reviewed the business calls she had to make when she went into the office on Monday. She was so lost in her thoughts, she didn't hear a girlish shout from behind until a pair of hands grasped her shoulders and sent her spinning into an ungraceful heap on the grass. Straining to catch her breath, Keri looked up at a young girl on roller skates gazing down at her with open concern.

"Gosh, I'm so sorry," the girl apologized, pushing waist-length dark brown hair away from her face. "I guess I sort of lost control. Are you okay?"

"I'm fine," Keri said when she was finally able to catch her breath.

"Lacy!" The angry male voice sent chills down Keri's spine.

Keri slowly turned her head and looked up. Ryan's eyes widened at the identity of Lacy's victim.

"Oh, my God," he groaned, dropping down on one knee and placing a hand on her shoulder. "Are you all right?" he demanded; then, without waiting for a reply, he looked up at the young girl. "Damnit, Lacy, how many times have I told you to be more careful on those things!" he roared, his dark brows drawn together in anger. "You could have seriously hurt this lady!"

"I'm sorry, Dad," she replied meekly, hanging her head in submission under the onslaught of his anger. "I picked up speed and couldn't stop."

Ryan turned back to Keri, who had sat open-mouthed during the exchange. Ryan had a teenage daughter?

"Are you all right?" he repeated, placing a gentle hand on her abdomen.

Keri felt a warming sensation through the thin cotton of her shirt. "I'm fine." Her voice was shaky as she struggled to sit upright.

"Any pain? Nausea? Cramps?" Ryan asked sharply, refusing to move his restraining hand to allow her to move just yet. He glanced up at his daughter with barely concealed rage on his face. "What I ought to do is turn

49

you over my knee, young lady, and give you the spanking you deserve for acting so carelessly."

"Please, don't blame her. I was daydreaming and I should have been more careful. I'm fine," Keri told him, wishing his face weren't so close to her own.

Ryan reached into the pocket of his warm-up jacket, withdrew a set of keys, and tossed them to Lacy. "Get the door," he ordered, while sliding an arm under Keri's legs and the other around her shoulders. "Then I want you to throw those damned skates in the trash!"

Glancing at her father's angry features and deciding that silence would be much safer, Lacy sped off.

"Please put me down," Keri pleaded, embarrassed. She had no option but to curl an arm around Ryan's neck as he straightened up. "I'm too heavy."

He grinned, showing a flash of white. "You aren't yet. Just don't try to jump into my arms a couple of months from now," he teased.

She drew a deep breath, then wished she hadn't as she inhaled the scent of his skin mixed with a tangy after-shave and perspiration. His navy athletic shorts and matching T-shirt indicated that he must have been out running. Where had he come from? It was obvious that he lived near there if he had given his daughter his keys and told her to go to the house.

"If you'll put me down, I can go home quite easily," she pointed out logically. "I don't live all that far from here."

"I live closer." Ryan carried her up a nearby walk and through an open door. He deposited her on a rust-colored tweed couch in a spacious living room decorated in chocolate and dark gold with touches of rust. "Lacy, fix some tea!" he commanded.

"I wouldn't be surprised if she left by way of the back door," Keri commented, looking around with interest. Why hadn't he mentioned his daughter when he talked about his divorce?

"Not if she wants to see her sixteenth birthday," he rumbled, staring down at Keri's pale face. "Are you sure you're all right?"

*"Yes!"* If he asked her that one more time, she'd scream!

A contrite Lacy, minus her roller skates and knee and elbow pads, appeared, carrying a steaming mug.

"Lacy, this is Miss Burke," Ryan introduced. "Keri, my daughter, Lacy."

"You're the one Dad took bowling last night." The young girl's smile lit her face up, then just as suddenly sobered. "I'm really sorry if I hurt you," she apologized again, handing Keri the mug.

"Contrary to your father's assumptions, I'm sturdier than I look." She sipped the comforting brew.

"Get lost." Ryan's command toward his daughter was tempered with love.

Keri flashed Lacy a reassuring smile. The girl's eyes were alarming duplicates of Ryan's but without the knowledge the man had gained over the years. Her long legs and overall likeness to a gangly filly suggested a teenager still growing. She had inherited a portion of her father's height, yet didn't seem intimidated by it, as many teenage girls would be. She would turn out to be a lovely woman in a few years, when all the rough edges of adolescence became smooth.

"I didn't know you lived here," Keri commented after Lacy had left the room.

"I knew you lived here before you told me," he said

softly, sitting down beside her. He grinned at her look of surprise. "I've seen you walk with someone who resembles a tenacious bulldog guarding his prize bone."

"Max," she explained, smiling at the apt description. The older man did tend to be overly protective. "He's my self-appointed mother hen: He reminds me about taking my vitamins, getting the proper amount of exercise, and eating balanced meals."

Ryan's eyes darkened. "The baby's father should be the one doing that."

Keri's hands shook, an action Ryan didn't miss, as she placed the mug on the coffee table in front of her. "I'm doing just fine, thank you."

"Does he know about the baby?" He continued his questioning, then asked in a gentle voice, "The baby's your ex-husband's, isn't it? Is that why you act troubled about your pregnancy?"

She flushed darkly, not wanting to discuss that subject with anyone, especially him. "I don't recall inviting the sharing of confidences," she said coolly.

"Doesn't he believe it's his?"

Not wanting to listen to any more of his interrogation, Keri jumped to her feet, then wished she hadn't, as a wave of nausea overtook her.

Ryan took in her distress and swiftly guided her to the bathroom. When her retching subsided, he wiped her face with a cool damp cloth and steered her upstairs. He directed her to a bedroom that faced the front. Ignoring her protests, he gently pushed her down onto the large bed, which moved beneath her. Keri's tennis shoes were removed and dropped onto the carpet, a quilt was draped over her, and a fluffed-up pillow was placed behind her head.

"Your morning sickness is a little late today," he teased gently, settling himself carefully on the edge of the bed while rubbing her clammy hands between his own.

"What morning sickness?" she moaned, closing her eyes. She was surprised that the gentle gyrations of the water bed were helping to diminish her nausea rather than increasing it. "I can have this any time of day, afternoon, or evening, and even in the middle of the night. The doctor who calls this morning sickness is out of his or her mind."

Ryan's brows knitted into a concerned frown. "Do you have this often?" he pressed.

"Enough," Keri said, sighing. She had never realized how comfortable a water bed could be. "If I tell you how embarrassed I feel about all this, will you pretend it never happened?" she murmured drowsily.

He gently pushed stray strands of hair away from her face. "It's kind of nice to see that you have your weak moments," he remarked idly, noting her eyelids drooping of their own accord. "I have an idea you slept as badly last night as I did."

"I have to go home," she protested weakly. "I have to clean the bathrooms." She felt too secure in the floating cocoon to move.

Ryan's low chuckle penetrated the pastel mists clouding Keri's mind. "I don't think you could clean a spoon, much less a bathroom. Sleep," he whispered, cupping her cheek with his palm.

It was enough to keep her a captive in those mists.

Ryan remained by Keri's side, watching her sleep.

"Dad?" Lacy's soft voice intruded on the quiet atmosphere.

He nodded, inclining his head toward her.

53

"Did I hurt her badly?" Alarm raced through her voice when she saw the sleeping figure.

He turned toward his daughter. "She's pregnant," he announced flatly.

"Oh." Now she really felt guilty. "Shouldn't we call her husband or something?"

It took him a moment to force the words out. "She doesn't have one."

"Oh." This response carried a wealth of understanding beyond her fifteen years. Lacy flipped back a loose lock of hair. "She's pretty." She watched her father's face with sharp eyes that resembled his.

"Yes," Ryan whispered, inwardly wishing that Keri were snaggletoothed and cross-eyed. It would make it all that much easier.

Keri stirred slowly and stretched. That's funny: The bed was rocking.

"Um," she mumbled, opening her eyes. "Oh!" She sat up, looking at the observer seated in a chair across the room.

"You're a very quiet sleeper." Ryan turned to extinguish his cigarette. He had since changed into a pair of cutoffs and a lemon-yellow T-shirt.

Keri felt uncomfortable knowing that he had watched her while she slept. It lent the situation an intimacy she didn't want it to have.

"Why can't you just leave things well enough alone?" she burst out. Her emotional well-being hadn't been too stable lately, as this flare-up proved. "Didn't you hear anything I said last night?" Her voice rose with her agitation.

Ryan now knew that Keri's short nap had revived her,

even if it was only her temper that had come back to life. She lay there looking vulnerable and so alone. By all rights she shouldn't arouse these protective feelings in him. At first he had been physically attracted to her and had wanted her in his bed. A bitter laugh threatened to erupt. Hell, she *was* in his bed! For all the good it did him. He had felt as if he had been kicked in the gut when she told him she was pregnant.

"I remember every word you told me that night. You're attracted to me, you don't think we should see each other, and you're pregnant," he said quietly. "Did I leave anything out?"

How could he just sit there so calmly? Keri wondered. Lately she either fluctuated on an unemotional plane or felt ready to scream at the slightest sound. The doctor said her erratic moods were due to her body's changes and would soon right themselves. It couldn't happen soon enough as far as she was concerned.

"Oh, you're awake." Lacy appeared in the doorway, then turned to Ryan. "Gina came over and wants to know if I can go swimming with her?"

"Meaning there's a bunch of boys out by the pool," he said wryly. "Sure, but be back by five."

She nodded, smiling at Keri. "I'm sorry you won't be able to go out to dinner with us tonight, Miss Burke," she said sincerely. "I hope I'll see you again next time without running you down." She blew a kiss, wiggled her fingers at Ryan, and left.

Keri's surprised eyes found his.

"Now you know that tonight would have been a threesome," he commented sardonically. "You would have accepted if you had known Lacy was coming, wouldn't you?"

"Another test?" she inquired.

Ryan's lips twitched. "It does seem to weed the ladies out, although they're more prone to turn me down when they hear that my daughter is coming along. A few have even made last-minute excuses when I've gone to pick them up."

"Does Lacy live with you all the time?" She found it difficult to imagine him as a full-time parent.

Ryan shook his head. He leaned forward, resting his elbows on his thighs. "I get her every other weekend and a month during the summer," he explained. The love he had for his daughter shone in his eyes.

"You must have married awfully young." She thought him to be in his mid-thirties, even with the silver frosting his dark hair.

Ryan smiled grimly as he said, "Stella got pregnant during our last year in college."

She hadn't expected him to be so open with her after her reticence about her past. "I'm sorry," she whispered.

"I don't regret Lacy." His austere features relaxed. "Although I don't know how any father can survive adolescence. She's fifteen going on forty, and at this rate I'll be a gray-haired old fool by the end of the year."

"Boys?" There was a mischievous tilt to her lips.

"Boys, new clothes, boys, makeup, boys, tennis, and more boys." He sighed, reaching up to massage the back of his neck.

Keri leaned over the side of the bed and groped for her shoes.

"Would you reconsider having dinner with us tonight, since you know Lacy will be present?" Ryan asked her abruptly.

"I don't think so," she replied softly, slipping her shoes

on and tying the laces. "I have to go to my sister's tomorrow, and I'm going to need every ounce of strength I have."

"Is she like you?"

"Amanda?" She laughed. "She's Attila the Hun, Genghis Khan, and Mother Goose all rolled up into one. If she can't run your life, she'll kill you with kindness. I really must go."

"I'll drive you home," he offered.

"It's only a short walk," she argued.

"Then I'll walk you home." He wasn't going to back down.

They were silent as they left the house. Keri spared a glance at the nearby golf course. Ryan obviously didn't have any money problems if he could live here. "Do you play?" she asked.

"Golf? It's too slow for me."

Keri would agree with him there. Now that she knew him better, she could see that he would prefer something faster-paced in which he could expend the great amounts of energy stored in his body.

When they reached her house, he entered without waiting for an invitation, as if he knew he wouldn't receive one.

"What are you doing?" Keri watched him climb the stairs, look in the room that she used as an office, then move down to her bedroom. She decided to find out for herself.

Ryan stood at her bedside table with her telephone in one hand, scribbling something on the attached emergency phone list. He set it down and turned back to her.

"My home and office numbers are on there," he told

her, capturing her eyes with his intent gaze. "If you need anything, I want you to call me."

"Why?" she couldn't resist asking.

"Because I want to be your friend," he said simply, keeping her eyes his prisoner.

"Do you honestly believe we can be friends?" Keri leaned against the doorjamb.

"I have an idea I'll be lucky if you'll just consider my request," he replied in a manner too candid for her taste. "You need a friend, Keri, and I don't mean that old man next door or a girl friend you go shopping with." His keen eyes skimmed over her, not missing one detail of her slightly disheveled appearance.

"You don't have to look at me as if I were some specimen under a microscope." She was feeling increasingly uneasy under his scrutiny.

"You're much too pale, your nausea shouldn't be as extreme as it is, and you're obviously working yourself too hard," he stated flatly, placing his hands on his hips, legs spread apart. "Are you trying purposely to lose your baby?"

"No!" Keri's denial came out fast and furious. "If I work too hard, it's because I have a business to run."

"That's what you have subordinates for," Ryan reminded her curtly. "Start delegating authority."

"What would you know about that?" she challenged, walking to the other side of the room. Belatedly she remembered he would know more about being in charge, a great deal more, than she did.

"I run my own business and you could say I have experienced pregnancy secondhand," he reminded her in a harsh voice.

Keri shook her head, wishing Ryan wouldn't badger

her so. Couldn't he see that she just couldn't handle any upsets right now?

"There's a big difference." She sighed. *"You* weren't the one to battle the nausea or the headaches or the mood swings. Also, your wife had someone there by her side when she needed comfort." Her eyes shimmered with tears. "And don't accuse me of feeling sorry for myself, because I'm not. I work because I have to and because there's no one else I can depend on but *me!*" She pointed her thumb against her chest for emphasis.

"You're wrong, Keri." He wanted nothing more than to walk across the room and take her into his arms. Hell, this woman was carrying another man's child, yet he wanted to ensure that she'd never be hurt. Why wasn't the other guy there, giving her the support she needed? One way or another he'd find out. "Are you sure you won't reconsider going out with us tonight?" he coaxed.

"Yes," she mumbled. Why couldn't he just leave her alone?

Ryan's sigh was audible across the room. "You realize, of course, that Lacy will be scared to death that I'll have *her* for dinner instead of a good steak."

It was a reluctant smile that came to her lips. "If she's anything like her father, she won't break down in front of an angry parent," she said lightly.

"True," he agreed with a grin. He looked around the room, pausing at the double bed with its lace-edged aquamarine comforter and matching pillow shams. A seascape hung over the bed. While the downstairs was decorated with the warm colors of the desert, the upstairs portrayed the cool surroundings of the sea, right down to a vanilla plush carpet resembling whitecaps on the ocean.

He wondered if she recognized the sensuality of the large dresser mirrors facing the bed.

He walked toward the doorway but stopped in front of a wary Keri. "I mean it, Keri." He wanted her to feel comfortable enough to rely on him in an emergency. "If you need me, you are to call me day or night and I'll be over here immediately."

"Even if you have . . . ah . . . company?" she couldn't resist asking.

Ryan wasn't laughing, though. "As hard as it may be for you to believe, I don't require a woman in my bed every night. I discovered a long time ago that casual sex is just that—meaningless and shallow. When I make love with a woman, it's more than a mutual desire for each other's bodies; it's a melding of the souls."

Keri stared up at him as if mesmerized. She was afraid to believe him. She was afraid of falling into another trap much more dangerous than the previous one she'd been caught in.

"I'll be interested in meeting your sister sometime," he said casually. His lean finger drew an imaginary line down her nose to her lips. When they probed past to her teeth, she could taste the salt on his skin. "I'll tell Lacy you'll have dinner with us on her next weekend with me." He placed his fingers against her lips to still her expected protest. "Perhaps I should call your sister and discover some of the tactics she uses to keep you in line," he mused.

"I think you're doing quite well on your own." She wished he wouldn't stand so close to her, or that he wasn't so magnetic, or . . .

"You get some rest," he advised. "No cleaning bathrooms! I'll see myself out."

Keri heard the click of the front door opening and closing. The news of her pregnancy hadn't shocked him as much as she had thought it would, or else he was able to hide his feelings well. No matter what, she couldn't see him as being content merely to be her friend. Ryan's impact on her today was much more forceful than it had been the night before—much more dangerous.

Late the next morning Keri drove to the outskirts of town, where many of the older and more expensive homes reigned over the city. Cal York, assistant district attorney and descendant of one of the founding fathers, owned one of the residences. It had been featured many times in well-known home-decorating magazines, thanks to the good taste of his wife, Amanda.

Amanda was just a little taller than Keri, her hair a golden brown cut in a chic short shag style; at thirty-seven her figure was every bit as toned as Keri's, due to regular workouts at her health club. She had a power of presence that could intimidate the strongest personality. No one would dare shorten her name to Mandy if they didn't want to fall victim to her icy demeanor.

"I like your outfit." Amanda greeted Keri with a hug, then stood back to study her sister's lacy antique blouse and solid lavender prairie skirt with a matching plaid ruffle circling the hem.

"Since it's fairly new, I figured I better wear it while I still can." Keri turned to hug her brother-in-law, who had just stepped out of the house. "Hello, Cal." Her voice was filled with warm affection for her sister's husband.

"Hi, lady." The tall man enveloped her in an immense bear hug that threatened to push all the air out of her.

Cal resembled a huge, lovable Saint Bernard, which usually lulled his opponents into thinking that they could easily defeat the mild-mannered man. Not so. In court Cal was sharp, decisive, and quick. It was a rare day when he lost a case.

"Aunt Keri!" Twin boys of eight ran out to do their own hugging.

"Hi, Randy and Roddy." She smiled affectionately at her nephews.

"All right, give her room." Amanda took charge and led Keri into the rambling ranch house. "Don't you have a barbecue to stand over?" She arched an eyebrow at her husband. "With you on the patio, the boys can go swimming and work off some of that energy they seem to always have in abundance."

"Yay!" The boys whooped and ran off before their mother could change her mind.

"Amanda, you should be in politics." Keri laughed, entering the shadowed interior of the house. "You'd have us lowly mortals whipped into shape in no time."

"I have enough trouble with all of you; I don't need any additional gray hairs." She was well used to her sister's good-natured teasing. "You look a little pale. Have you been getting enough rest? Are you remembering to take your vitamins? Are you exercising properly? You know how important that is, not only for your own health but for your baby's too." Amanda knew that there had never been any question of Keri having an abortion or giving the child up for adoption. Keri saw nothing wrong in being a single mother. Amanda was determined that her younger sister have all the love she and Keri's friends could provide her.

"Yes, yes, and yes." Keri followed Amanda into the

large, sunny kitchen. She sat on one of the stools at the breakfast bar and watched her older sister take a copper pan from the circular hanging rack over the stove. "Didn't Max call you with his weekly progress report?" she couldn't resist asking slyly.

"I called him Friday evening. He told me you were going out that evening." She couldn't miss her younger sister's faintly flushed features. "He said it was with a client."

"That's right," Keri replied noncommittally.

Amanda filled a tall glass with iced tea and placed it and a plate of cookies in front of Keri.

"The tea is herbal—no caffeine—and the cookies are from a new recipe. There isn't any sugar in them," she explained.

"Sounds perfectly disgusting." Keri wrinkled her nose but tried one. She wasn't surprised to find they were good. She doubted that any recipe Amanda tried didn't come out. It just wouldn't dare! She loved her sister dearly and was used to her loving but domineering ways, and no one would dare say anything against Amanda within Keri's hearing. But just once she wished Amanda would make one tiny mistake!

"How was your date?"

"It wasn't a date," Keri denied calmly.

"The client was a man?" Amanda handed Keri a loaf of French bread and butter with instructions to prepare it for warming.

"Yes." Keri knew exactly where the interrogation was heading. At times like this she wondered if it shouldn't have been Amanda who had gone into law. She would have made a great trial lawyer.

"Young, good-looking, single?" Amanda continued.

"Mid-thirties, well preserved for his age. He's divorced and has his fifteen-year-old daughter every other weekend." She bit into one of the buttered slices of bread, receiving a glare from Amanda. "I'm hungry! His name's Ryan Kincaid."

"Kincaid?" Cal walked in at the tail end of their conversation. "The land broker?"

"That's right. He's using one of my secretaries," Keri explained, still not willing to volunteer too much information. Amanda hadn't liked Larry from the start, and the feeling had been mutual. Of course, she hadn't liked Don, either, although Keri had a sneaking suspicion that Ryan could hold his own very easily with Amanda.

Cal and Amanda exchanged glances. "A tough businessman," he commented. "He and Jason Caldwell have gone far in the past ten years. I've never heard anything negative about him."

"Does he know you're pregnant?" Amanda asked bluntly.

Keri heaved a deep sigh. "He's a client, Amanda, nothing more. And yes, he knows."

"Have you called Don and told him about the baby yet?" Cal asked her gently.

She shook her head. "There's no reason to do that." She was beginning to feel weary, as if this were Pick-on-Keri Day. "I very much doubt that I'll be seeing him again." She turned to Amanda, wanting to get off the subject of her ex-husband. "If it would make you feel any better, Ryan Kincaid did express an interest in meeting you."

"He did?" She looked suspicious. "I don't think I have to warn you to be cautious."

Keri shook her head. "There's no room in my life for

any man." She wrapped the buttered bread in aluminum foil and set it aside.

"I hope you told him who your brother-in-law is," Amanda said forcefully.

"I don't think it would faze him one bit; besides, I think he'd feel more intimidated by you," she teased, secretly doubting that would ever happen. In a battle of wills, she had a pretty good idea that Ryan would come out the winner.

Amanda glared at Keri. "You all make me sound like some kind of tyrant," she accused her sister and husband.

"That's only because you are, my love. That's all right; I adore you anyway." Cal's face and eyes crinkled into an affectionate smile as he bestowed a warm kiss on Amanda's lips. For a moment they were lost in their own murmurings.

"Fondling in the kitchen again!" Keri teased, while inwardly wishing she could partake of this same kind of love. She knew she never would, though. She could only sit back and observe and hide her pain.

## CHAPTER FOUR

It didn't take Keri long to find out exactly how persistent Ryan Kincaid could be.

He called her at seven on Monday morning. She hung up before he got past telling her his name. He called her at the office not long after her arrival. She told Serena to tell him she was on another line.

She handed the Kincaid account over to Barb with the explanation that she didn't have the time to handle it.

Ryan insisted on Keri's personal service. Keri said that if he wouldn't settle for Barb, he could use another agency and lose Cassie.

Ryan called again that evening. This time when Keri hung up, she left the phone off the hook. When there was a knock on her door fifteen minutes later, she ignored it.

"What is going on between you and Mr. Kincaid?" Barb demanded on Tuesday morning.

"Nothing," Keri muttered. What was he trying to pull now? Couldn't he see that she wanted nothing to do with him?

"That's not true as far as he's concerned," she continued. "He asked me if you were eating properly and if you were feeling all right." She gazed at Keri suspiciously.

"Why can't he just leave me alone!" she wailed, sinking into her chair.

"He genuinely cares about you, Keri. Just the way we do," Barb reproved.

"So does my mother, but she knows enough to stay out of my personal life," Keri muttered, pushing a stray lock of hair out of her face. "Why can't he take a hint that I don't want him around me?"

The other woman looked at her as if she were crazy not to want a devilishly handsome man like Ryan Kincaid hovering around her. It was obvious that he knew about her pregnancy and that it didn't matter. Or if it did, he still cared more about the woman.

"If you're that adamant about the man staying away from you, why don't you just come out and tell him so?" Barb suggested before walking out of the office. "Although if you do, you'll be one very sorry young woman."

Keri continued taking the coward's way out instead. She hated to admit that she was afraid of the feelings Ryan generated in her.

She bought a telephone answering machine and hooked it up at home. She received an average of four calls a day from Ryan.

"Keri, I want to talk to you." He used his authoritative voice.

"I know you're there, Keri, so pick up this phone!" Exasperation.

"Damnit to hell, Keri, talk to me!" His temper was now beginning to show.

And then: "Keri baby, don't do this. Let's talk about whatever is bothering you."

Keri listened to each message with her hands clenched at her sides. Then she flipped on the Quick Erase switch.

Late that Friday morning Keri was looking over the

weekly billing. The hairs prickling along her nape were her first warning.

"You're a stubborn woman, Keri Burke," Ryan declared. He placed his palms in front of her on her desk.

She slowly raised her eyes. "Barb is handling your account now, Mr. Kincaid," she said formally, ignoring the churning in her stomach, which had nothing to do with morning sickness.

There was a dark flicker in Ryan's eyes. "You look like hell," he stated bluntly. "You look like you've lost weight, and there isn't one trace of that glow pregnant women are supposed to have."

"I guess I shouldn't expect flowery compliments from a man who takes a woman bowling and out for pizza," Keri injected dryly.

Ryan spun around to face an open-mouthed Serena. "I'm taking your boss to lunch." There was no mistaking that authoritative tone.

"No you're not," Keri argued without hesitation. "I've already eaten," she lied.

"No you haven't," Serena protested, ignoring the glare directed her way.

"Who's paying the salaries around here?" Keri threatened.

"If you keep on going the way you are, the only thing you'll be paying is a hospital bill." Ryan hunted through Keri's desk drawers until he found her purse. "Here, I'm sure you won't feel well dressed without it."

"I'm not going anywhere with you." She continued to argue even as he pulled her to her feet and propelled her out of the office.

"We'll be back in about an hour and a half," Ryan tossed over his shoulder while pushing Keri out the door.

Lunch was a quiet affair. Keri ate her meal in a stony silence.

"There's no getting away from me, Keri," Ryan told her when he dropped her off at her office.

She smiled frostily. "Don't place any bets on it, Ryan."

"I don't need to. I always win." With that, he grinned and drove off.


Keri's morning sickness hit her with a vengeance just before dawn on Monday. As soon as she felt it was safe to leave the bathroom for more than two minutes, she called Barb and explained that she'd be late coming to the office.

"You call the doctor and tell him how bad the nausea is," Barb ordered. "It's wearing you out, Keri. There's medication you can take for morning sickness."

"He doesn't believe in too much medication for expectant mothers." Keri sighed, then felt the familiar rumblings in her stomach. "I'll call you later." She hung up and ran for the bathroom.

When the nausea subsided sufficiently, Keri went downstairs for a few soda crackers and a cup of tea. She curled up on the couch, feeling as if she had been tortured on a rack for the past few years.

Keri groaned when the doorbell rang. "Go away," she pleaded with the unseen caller.

Instead the person ignored her plea and merely continued his efforts by pounding on the door.

"Keri, open up!" Ryan's command vibrated through the house.

Keri groaned again. *Terrific. He would show up when I resemble something out of a horror film.*

69

"Keri, so help me, I'll call the police!" Ryan threatened.

She couldn't ignore him because she knew only too well he would carry out his threat.

"All right, but you asked for it," Keri muttered, slowly rising to her feet and heading for the door. While she expected to find an angry Ryan on the front step, she hadn't expected him also to look pale and very worried.

"I've seen drowned cats who looked better," he said as he brushed past her and walked into the living room.

"Thank you for the compliment," she snapped, only too aware of her wrinkled pink cotton robe and her hair hanging in lackluster strands around her face and pasty features. "You've made my day. Now perhaps you can tell me what you're doing here."

"I called your office to see if you would have lunch with me one day this week, and your receptionist said you were home sick." Ryan studied Keri closely. "Morning sickness again?"

Keri nodded wearily and collapsed onto the couch again.

Ryan frowned. He walked over to Keri and placed his hand on her forehead.

"You don't have a temperature," he muttered. "But your skin feels clammy. If the nausea is this bad, why aren't you taking medication? Or are you too stubborn to allow yourself to feel better?" he asked sardonically.

"I'm not that stupid." Keri rested her head against the back of the couch. "My doctor doesn't believe in too much medication in the early stages of pregnancy. He's assured me that the nausea will be gone soon." Swearing hard and long, Ryan paced the length of the living room.

"Ryan, please, I have a headache," Keri begged, surprised at her own plaintive tone of voice.

"What's your doctor's name?" Ryan snapped.

"None of your business. Now, please go away!"

He walked into the kitchen, rummaged through the notebooks by the phone, then decided to take matters into his own hands. With a horrified expression on her face, Keri listened to him dial the phone and ask for Barb.

"Hello, Barb, this is Ryan Kincaid." He was charm personified. "I'm over at Keri's house and she's acting too stubborn for her own good. What's her doctor's name? Whether he likes it or not, he's going to prescribe something for this nausea of hers."

Keri groaned audibly. "Oh, Barb, please don't tell him," she whispered.

"Dr. Chalmers." Ryan smiled as he heard Keri's threats against her employee. "Thank you. Yes, I'll take care of her."

"No!" Keri moaned loudly.

But Ryan wasn't finished. Keri sat huddled in the corner of the couch, listening to him call her doctor's office and demand an appointment for her.

"I'll never live this down," she muttered, watching him walk back into the living room.

"You have an appointment in an hour," he brusquely informed her. "I'll drive you over to your doctor's office." Whether she wanted him to or not was left unasked and unsaid. "Do you need help getting dressed?" There was no male leer accompanying the question.

Keri rose slowly to her feet. "No, thank you," she murmured. "Since you've already made yourself at home,

71

you may as well feel free to make yourself some coffee." She headed for the stairs.

A warm shower and shampoo helped restore Keri's equilibrium. She blew her hair dry and piled it on top of her head and applied a light layer of makeup, which wasn't able to restore a healthy color to her skin or a bright glow to her eyes. She pulled her robe on and walked back into her bedroom.

She didn't expect to find Ryan lounging in the wicker chair by the window.

"I said to make yourself at home in the living room, not up here," Keri said tartly, stepping back in surprise.

"I wanted to make sure that you were all right."

Keri eyed Ryan narrowly. She didn't want to trust him. He was a man and men inflicted pain.

Ryan instantly noted her withdrawal. "I was afraid you might become ill again, Keri," he explained softly, standing up. "I'll go downstairs."

"Perhaps *he* should go to the doctor instead of me," Keri muttered, reaching into the closet for clean clothes and dressing quickly in jeans and a pale pink T-shirt. When Keri returned downstairs, Ryan looked up from the magazine he was leafing through.

"Would you like a cup of tea before we leave?" he asked politely.

Keri shook her head. "I can certainly drive myself, if you're so insistent that I see the doctor."

Ryan grinned crookedly. "Far be it that I allow a sick woman to drive herself to the doctor. That wouldn't be the gentlemanly thing to do."

"Why not?"

He stood up and rummaged in his slacks pocket for his car keys. "Isn't that what friends are for? You need someone to help you when you aren't feeling well, and I'm here."

"Why can't you just leave well enough alone?" Keri asked Ryan as he led her outside and to his car. "I was doing just fine before you appeared."

"Sure, upchucking breakfast, lunch, and dinner. That's really doing fine," Ryan retorted, handing Keri a small sandwich bag filled with soda crackers. "Just in case."

Keri grimaced. Oh, yes, Ryan was definitely well versed in pregnancy symptoms.

"I hate men who are always well prepared," she informed him with a faint curl of the lip.

"Part of my Boy Scout training," he said, unperturbed by her bad mood.

Keri waited for Ryan to ask for directions, but he must have gotten some from the doctor's receptionist because he drove to the medical center without any trouble.

"I shouldn't be long." Keri reached for the door handle as soon as Ryan had parked the car.

"I'm tagging along," he told her firmly, pushing his own door open.

Keri froze. "You can't do that!" she nearly shrieked.

Ryan placed a casual arm around her shoulders and guided her to the entrance.

"Sure I can."

"No, you *can't!*" Keri hissed.

"Sure. It's easy. I walk over to suite 106 with you, open the door, and enter," Ryan stated calmly, finding the correct door and opening it.

Keri could have died of embarrassment when she entered the doctor's reception area with Ryan following closely behind.

Four women, all in various stages of pregnancy,

73

watched Keri walk toward the reception desk as Ryan settled himself in a nearby chair. She gave her name to the receptionist, then had no choice but to take the empty chair next to Ryan's.

"Your first?" one of the women asked Ryan with a smile.

"I have a fifteen-year-old daughter," Ryan replied easily.

Keri buried her face in a magazine while Ryan questioned the woman about her pregnancy and her opinion of Dr. Chalmers.

*I hadn't planned on going to the breakfast that morning,* Keri thought to herself. *From now on, I'll always follow my hunches. If I had, I could be at home now, playing invalid.*

A nurse appeared in the open doorway. "Mrs. Baxter."

A heavily pregnant woman struggled to her feet.

Ryan looked around the office with genuine interest. "So this is what an obstetrician's office looks like," he commented.

"Ryan, please," Keri pleaded under her breath.

"I'm just curious, that's all," he replied with bland innocence.

Ryan wasn't finished with Keri by a long shot. When Keri's name was called, Ryan also stood up.

"What are you doing?" she demanded in a whisper.

"If that doctor believes that your nausea will go away soon, I want to hear him say so."

"You have no business going in there," Keri snapped.

Ryan's eyes glowed darkly. "Then I'll just make it my business, won't I?"

Dr. Chalmers greeted Keri's companion with surprise, and Ryan didn't look overly impressed with the elderly

74

medical man after he discussed Keri's severe bouts of nausea.

"Tell me, Mr. Kincaid, are you the baby's father?" Dr. Chalmers asked bluntly.

"No, but I am a good friend of Keri's."

Dr. Chalmers nodded. *That* kind of friend, was he? "Morning sickness is a common symptom associated with pregnancy, Mr. Kincaid," he said in a condescending voice. "Once Ms. Burke gets into the second trimester, she'll be the picture of health."

"Then she's got a long way to go." Ryan didn't appear pleased by the doctor's diagnosis. "Her employees say she's sick more than well and she's become a very light eater. I also understand she has trouble sleeping."

Keri sat there wondering if her face looked as red as it felt. How dare Ryan do this to her! Before he finished, Keri had a prescription to treat her nausea and a more thoughtful Dr. Chalmers listening to her.

"I have never been so mortified in my life," she muttered between clenched teeth when she was again seated in his Porsche an hour later.

Ryan shook his head in wonderment. "The man is still back in the Dark Ages." He leaned forward and inserted the key in the ignition, switching the engine on. "He'd be the type who wouldn't allow medication during the delivery either."

"Natural childbirth is in style," Keri reminded him.

"Where did you get his name?" he asked curiously.

"Max plays poker with Dr. Chalmers," she replied wearily. It had been a long morning.

"How long has *he* known him?"

Keri sighed. "Fifteen years."

Ryan expelled a sharp breath. "Terrific!" he said, slap-

75

ping the steering wheel with his open palm. He turned in his seat and captured Keri's nape with gentle fingers. "Keri, I want you to do me two favors."

She stared at him warily. "What?"

A muscle worked in the corner of his mouth. "First, I'd like you to find a different doctor—one who's more patient-oriented; and second, tell the father about the baby."

Keri whitened until her eyes stood out like rare jewels in her face. For a moment Ryan was afraid she'd faint.

"Take me home," she demanded between stiff lips. "Now."

"Keri . . ." Ryan began, but anything he was about to say was sliced away by a swift shake of Keri's head.

"No more." Her voice shook with fury, or was it fear? "I want to go home, Ryan."

He turned away and put the car in gear. The silence between them was thick with tension during the drive back to Keri's condo. Ryan had barely stopped the car when Keri opened the door and jumped out.

"I'll thank you for taking me to the doctor, but that's all." Her voice was now cold and emotionless. "I've asked you before, but now I'm demanding it: Stay out of my life, Ryan. I've gotten along fine for thirty-one years without you, so I expect I can do quite well for the next thirty-one. *I don't want you in my life!*" Her eyes glimmered with unshed tears. She stepped back, slammed the door shut, and ran to the front door.

Ryan made no attempt to follow her. He knew that her emotional state couldn't handle a confrontation just now, so he would just bide his time. Whether it be business or personal, he could be extremely patient when necessary.

According to local business gossip, Ryan was a hard-hearted SOB. He allowed nothing to get in the way of business. People who dealt with him on a professional level claimed that his company was all he needed in his life. Very few people knew that Ryan did have a soft spot —his daughter.

Lacy was a very important part of Ryan's private life. She had always been able to twist him around her little finger unless her requests were too outlandish. Ryan could be only a part-time father, but he refused to buy her love with material goods. Lacy meant everything to him, and he would do anything to ensure her happiness.

Then there was Keri. Ryan knew she was an independent and self-sufficient woman, and he admired her for those traits. At the same time, he felt she should have someone to lean on. It wasn't Ryan's chauvinistic side asserting itself; he just felt that Keri should have a helping hand when the time came.

Ryan's stomach churned. By all rights he should follow Keri's plea and leave her alone. After all, she *was* pregnant, and it had nothing to do with him.

"I almost wish it did," he muttered tightly, pressing his foot down on the accelerator. "Damn, why can't I let her go?"

Ryan couldn't help but wonder about the father of Keri's baby. What had happened to the man who had gotten Keri pregnant? Why did she refuse to talk about the man? Had she been—? Ryan's blood ran cold at the idea of any kind of violence inflicted on Keri.

By the time Ryan's thoughts returned to the present, he found himself on the city outskirts—with no knowledge of how he had gotten there. As soon as he could, he turned the car around and drove back into town and toward his office. He had a great deal of work to do.

Keri spent the rest of the day taking it easy. She left the house only once, to drive to the pharmacy to have her prescription filled. After following the directions on the small brown bottle of tablets, she found the nausea subsiding and eventually disappearing.

Keri drank her hot tea and kept watching her silent telephone all evening. Obviously Ryan had taken her at her word and wasn't going to try to contact her again. That was what she wanted, wasn't it? Then why did it hurt so? Did the idea of her being pregnant bother him after all?

After the trauma she had suffered because of Larry, Keri shouldn't want anything to do with a man. Yet, she knew that if she had met Ryan six months earlier, it wouldn't have taken much for them to become lovers. Part of her wanted to pick up the phone and call him to apologize for her harsh words. The other part told her that it was for the best and she would be better off. She'd be responsible for herself; that way there would be no pain.

"You're looking a little peaked, lass," Max chided Keri during their walk two evenings later. "You're still taking your vitamins, aren't you?"

"Like clockwork," she replied dryly, taking the elderly man's arm.

"Dr. Chalmers said you had a man with you when you saw him," he commented casually.

"Mr. Kincaid is a very insistent man when it comes to having his own way," Keri murmured.

"Sounds like the kind of man you need," Max went on.

"You're more than enough for me," she teased, rapidly

78

changing the subject. "So how many suckers did you fleece during your poker game?"

They continued walking down the lamplit sidewalk and talking softly.

"Keri."

She looked up and saw Ryan standing under a lamp. Max studied a surprised Keri and a watchful Ryan.

"If it's all right with you, sir, I'll see Keri home." Ryan spoke respectfully to the older man.

"Wellll . . ." Max deliberated. He wagged a warning finger at Ryan. "You have her back safe and sound, young man, or I'll know who to find."

"No one has asked me if I want him to take me home," Keri muttered, although the light in her eyes said something different.

Ryan swung back to Keri. "Please?" His dark eyes emphasized his plea. He held out a hand.

"I'll be going on home." As Max walked past he gave Keri a gentle shove in Ryan's direction. She stumbled slightly but regained her balance.

Ryan crossed the short distance separating him from Keri. "If it will make you feel better, I'll discuss Cassie's faults." He grinned. "That puts our discussion on a business footing."

"Cassie has no faults!" Keri retorted indignantly.

"That was a quick discussion, wasn't it?"

Keri's lips twitched with suppressed laughter. "You're incorrigible."

"Only where you're concerned." He brushed a strand of stray hair away from her face. "Don't be afraid of me, Keri. I'd never hurt you."

"Never make promises you can't keep." She backed away from his caressing hand.

"My place is only a few steps from here. How about something to drink?" Ryan asked.

Keri shook her head and took another step back.

Ryan sighed. Why did he have to fall for one of the most obstinate women around?

"Is it all right if I walk you home, then?"

Keri searched Ryan's face for sarcasm but found none. "All right."

During the short walk back to Keri's condo, Ryan walked alongside her but made no move to touch her.

"Has the medication been helping your nausea?" he asked.

"Yes, thank you." She looked down, concentrating on putting one foot in front of the other instead of thinking about the musky tang of Ryan's clean scent. She braved a brief glance at his profile. What had prompted him to appear so suddenly? She found the nerve to put her thought into words and waited for his reply.

"I wanted to see you again," he answered simply. "I just wasn't sure if you'd speak to me or ignore me."

Keri didn't know how she felt either. When they reached her front door, she fumbled in her shorts pocket for her keys.

"May I come in if I stay for one cup of coffee and nothing else?" Ryan pleaded. "Please, Keri?"

She shook her head, wishing he wasn't quite so charming. "Now I can see why you've done so well in your business. You kill your victims with charm." She pushed the door open and walked inside. When she entered the kitchen, she switched on a light.

"Do you—?" She spun around, only to find Ryan a breath away. She cleared her throat and said huskily, "I have some doughnuts, if you'd like something to go with your coffee." The trouble was, she had a very clear idea of *what* he wanted with his coffee, and it wasn't doughnuts!

"Sounds good to me, but should you be eating them?" he asked.

"Probably not, but when they're filled with Bavarian cream and smothered with chocolate, I'm in heaven." Keri hurriedly set up the coffee maker. Her kitchen suddenly seemed very small with Ryan standing so close to her.

"Where are your plates and the doughnuts? The least I can do is help you," he offered.

Keri pointed in the direction of the pantry. She could hear cabinet doors opening and closing. She tensed every time she heard Ryan taking a step, half afraid he might try to touch her and half hoping he would.

"Do you take cream or sugar?" she asked.

"I take it black." He set the plates on the round ice-cream-parlor–style table and sat in a blue-and-white-striped chair with a scrolled wrought-iron back. "It must be hard to keep your plants from drying out, what with the sun and heat," he commented, glancing out the window at the small patio.

Keri nodded as she set down two mugs filled with coffee, hers a pale brown from the cream she had added to her own mug. "My water bill is horrendous." She laughed, taking the chair across from Ryan. She picked up a doughnut and bit into it, an expression of bliss on her face upon tasting the rich filling. "Umm."

"Something tells me that you have a touch of the hedonist in you," Ryan teased.

Keri's features froze. "Yes, so I've been told," she replied stiffly.

Ryan's eyes narrowed. He took a sip of the hot coffee and set the mug down. "I get the impression that you aren't exactly enamored with the male sex." He cocked his head to one side as he studied her stony expression. "And right now you aren't too happy with yourself because you're physically attracted to me."

"I shouldn't be!" she moaned, not bothering to refute his statement.

"Keri, it's perfectly natural," Ryan said softly. "You're a normal, red-blooded woman."

"Please, could we talk about something else?"

Ryan sighed. "Do you think it will go away if you ignore it, Keri? Did you think that your baby would disappear the same way?" he added ruthlessly.

Keri refused to give in to the tears that threatened to overtake her. "If I'm such a horrible person, why do you keep coming back?" she challenged.

"Damned if I know," he grumbled, picking up a second doughnut and biting into it.

"I could stay mad at you longer if you would just remain some kind of monster longer," Keri retorted.

Ryan flashed her a wicked grin. "I've been told more than once what a heartless bastard I am."

"It's because you look like one." Keri breathed in sharply and clapped her hand over her mouth. Whatever had possessed her to say that? "I—I mean—"

"Hey, it's okay," he consoled her. "I'm well aware that I possess an excellent face for playing poker. I can also look like someone no man in his right mind would try to fool with. But it's a trade secret that underneath this granite exterior is a cuddly old teddy bear."

Ryan could see the smile working its way along the

corner of Keri's mouth. "Teddy bear?" She arched a skeptical eyebrow.

"Just don't tell Lacy. I have enough trouble with that kid as it is."

"She's a lucky girl to have you for a father," Keri said sincerely. "When my parents divorced, my father decided his latest girl friend was more important than his daughter."

Ryan couldn't miss the bitterness in her voice. "How old were you when your parents divorced?"

"Old enough to feel relieved that there wouldn't be any more fights," she replied. "Would you like more coffee?" she asked, desperate to change the subject.

He smiled, knowing what she was doing. "No, thanks. I should get going." He rose to his feet.

Keri followed Ryan to the door. Before he opened it, he turned around and put his hands on her shoulders. "I'd like to take you out this weekend, Keri," he said softly.

"Pregnant women don't go out on dates."

"This pregnant lady can. Nothing fancy," Ryan assured her. "We'll keep it all casual." *And nonthreatening,* he silently added.

She looked up at him from under slightly lowered lashes in a manner that was more mischievous than provocative. "No bowling."

Ryan drew an easy breath. "No bowling. I'll pick you up at six-thirty on Friday night."

"It's all wrong, Ryan," Keri blurted out. "You're the kind of man who needs a woman in the physical sense, and I won't have an affair with you. I'm not the kind of woman you need or would want."

"Don't tell me what kind of woman I need or want,

Keri Burke," Ryan chided softly. He picked up her hand and placed a gentle kiss in her palm. "I'll see you Friday night."

Keri saw the front door open and close and heard Ryan's footsteps on the walkway. Her palm tingled where his lips had placed the tender kiss.

"I know what you need and want, Ryan Kincaid," she whispered. "Because, God help me, I have the same needs."

## CHAPTER FIVE

Keri was rapidly discovering that Ryan was a man of surprises.

"You weren't kidding about another casual date, were you?" She looked around the miniature golf course with its castles and moats, clocktowers and clowns, denoting the course holes. A glance told her that she and Ryan were the oldest couple present, with the average age of the players in the mid- to late teens. "I'll have you know that I haven't gone miniature golfing on a date since I was twelve."

"Twelve?" Ryan frowned. "Isn't that a little young to date?"

"Not when you're part of a group and the boy was an elderly thirteen." Keri chose an orange golf ball, leaving a blue one for Ryan. "I'm going to beat the pants off you," she declared loftily.

"I'd love it," Ryan purred in her ear, then laughed out loud when Keri blushed furiously.

During the course of their play, Keri discovered another side to Ryan. Perhaps it was having a fifteen-year-old daughter that enabled him to remain patient despite the antics of the teenagers playing before and after them. Two couples were playing ahead of them, with the boys showing off for their girl friends, complete with the usual kidding around. Keri waited her turn and thought nothing of Ryan's arm draped casually over her shoulders.

"Mad at me?" His warm breath stirred the stray hairs at her temples.

She smiled and shook her head. "I'm having a lot of fun." Unconsciously she leaned against him.

"I'm glad." Ryan planted a light kiss above her brow and gave her a gentle shove. "It's your turn."

Keri looked up and laughed as she hadn't in a long time. Ryan observed her free manner and breathed easier. Perhaps she was finally beginning to trust him.

Keri studied the difficult approach. The ball would have to hit a certain spot against the low wall, then curve around a painted snake's body before it would even have a chance of rolling near the hole.

"Take your time," Ryan advised in a low voice.

Keri took a deep breath, closed her eyes, swung the golf club back, and brought it forward. A tiny *crack!* sounded in the air. She opened one eye slightly to watch the tiny ball's progress. Her mouth dropped open when the ball rolled neatly into the hole.

"I got a hole in one!" she screamed, jumping up and down. "I got a hole in one!" She threw her arms around Ryan's neck and hugged him tightly. She drew back slightly and, standing still, saw a strange expression in his dark eyes. For a moment the world receded into a hazy mist and they became the only inhabitants in the cloudy haven.

"Damn you, Keri," Ryan groaned, finally breaking the spell. "Why do you have to go all soft and sexy in the middle of this zoo?"

Keri flushed and stepped back. She hurriedly walked over to the hole and retrieved her ball.

For the rest of the game Ryan's playing went to pieces. He was too busy remembering the feel of Keri's body against his and the scent of her perfume filling his nostrils. It was difficult to concentrate when he could see how Keri's full breasts strained against her powder-blue short-sleeved cotton sweater and how her derriere was outlined by her white cotton pants.

"Think you've worked up an appetite?" Ryan asked after he had totaled up both scores. Keri had won by a mile.

"Chinese?" she asked hopefully as they turned in their golf clubs.

Ryan laughed, circling Keri's shoulders with his arm. "Chinese it is."

A little over an hour later a stunned Ryan sat back and watched Keri eat cashew chicken, sweet-and-sour pork, deep-fried shrimp, egg rolls, wonton, and pork fried rice. It wasn't until she began nibbling on an almond cookie and sipped her tea that he spoke.

"Get enough?" he teased lightly.

Keri's cheeks turned a deep rose. "I can't believe I ate so much," she apologized.

"Hey, I like to see a woman enjoy her food," he assured her, handing her a fortune cookie.

"No use in worrying about my figure," she muttered, then stiffened. Why had she brought her pregnancy up? She broke the fortune cookie open and unrolled the tiny piece of paper.

" 'You needn't cross the sea to find home,' " Ryan read his fortune out loud. "Good, I get seasick too easily. What's yours?" He looked up and saw the dismay written on her face. "Keri?"

"It's all nonsense," she said, crumpling the paper in

87

her hand and dropping it on her plate. "Would you please excuse me for a moment?" She hurriedly left the booth.

Ryan watched Keri disappear in the direction of the restrooms before he leaned over and picked up the paper.

*The pain will be short, the joy forever,* he read to himself.

Ryan replaced the small piece of paper on the plate and leaned back in his chair. Why would those few words upset her so much that she had to run away? He wondered if Keri would ever trust him enough to confide her troubles to him. He knew he was lucky that she allowed him close to her at all. He had even called on her old pug, Max, but the elderly man wouldn't talk about Keri. Oh, he had said that she was a lovely and kind lady, but he had refused to discuss Keri any further. If Ryan wanted to know more about her, he would have to ask her himself.

When Keri returned to the table, Ryan could see that a new layer of blusher and a deep-pink gloss had been reapplied to her cheeks and lips.

"I've already taken care of the check if you want to leave," Ryan informed her quietly.

"All right." She managed a weak smile.

When they had finally settled themselves in his low-slung Porsche, Keri turned to Ryan.

"Ryan"—she laid her hand on his arm—"I'm sorry; I don't know what's wrong with me anymore. I swear, if someone looks at me cross-eyed, I break down in tears."

He nodded in understanding. "Hormones. They'll straighten out soon."

"Don't be so nice to me!" Keri wailed.

"Okay, honey, I'll try to yell at you more often," he agreed matter-of-factly, which only made Keri wail louder. Ryan sighed with relief. Ironic as it was, he figured that she just might be back to normal, and he was glad that she was cranky. He switched the engine on.

"Do you have any doughnuts left?" Ryan asked when he pulled up in front of Keri's condo.

"With Chinese food?" She wrinkled her nose with distaste at the food combination. "I guess you're inviting yourself inside again."

"You don't seem to want to invite me in, so I have to take the initiative," Ryan replied, getting out of the car and walking around to the passenger door to assist Keri.

"Perhaps I have a reason," Keri said tartly, rummaging in her purse for her keys.

"Your air conditioning doesn't work? True, I guess I wouldn't come in then." He followed her inside. "Don't worry about waiting on me; I can help myself."

Keri curled up on the couch and listened to Ryan rattle around in the kitchen. "If you make a mess, you'll have to clean it up," she called out.

"Don't worry, I'm a very neat person," he called back. "You've got three doughnuts left. Want one?"

"No, thank you." Keri slipped off her shoes and tucked her feet underneath herself. "But since you're asking, I will have some iced tea."

"Lemon or sugar?"

"No."

Ryan came out of the kitchen carrying a teak tray with two glasses of tea and the three doughnuts. He set the tray on the coffee table and then turned on the stereo before sitting down beside her.

"I think you've gotten me hooked on these things." Ryan bit into the cream-filled pastry.

"The shop is around the corner from my office, so I

usually get some on my way home." Keri picked up her glass of tea.

Ryan made short work of the three doughnuts and drank half of his iced tea. He slid closer to Keri and took the glass out of her hand, placing it on the coffee table. He framed her face with his hands, forcing her to look directly at him.

"Now, listen to me carefully, Keri," he ordered softly. "I'm going to kiss you and I don't want you to feel frightened. It's only a kiss," he whispered against her quivering lips.

His cool lips touched her in a fleeting caress, then returned to increase the pressure.

Keri's head whirled. This was *only* a kiss? At first she stiffened, but Ryan didn't try to deepen the kiss or touch her anywhere else. His closed lips continued to brush over hers in light caresses. When he felt her relaxing, he slid his arms around her and pulled her closer against him. He placed tiny nibbles along Keri's jaw and at the corners of her mouth.

"You're very lovely, Keri," he whispered, now mapping out the whirls in her ear with the tip of his tongue.

"P-please stop," she begged suddenly, finding his kisses too much for her.

Ryan pulled back. His lean forefinger traced the dampness under her eyes. "I don't want you to be afraid of me, love," he said softly, looking down at the salty moisture on his fingers. "I'd never hurt you."

Keri inhaled sharply. "Are—are you saying that you'd stop now just because I've asked you to?" she questioned.

Ryan nodded. Keri's eyes bored into his sable-colored ones.

"I-if you kissed me again and I asked you to stop, you

would?" she asked in a small voice that wobbled. "And— and you wouldn't think that I was a tease?"

"You aren't the kind of woman to lead a man on deliberately." He allowed his thumbs to draw imaginary circles on her neck. "If you tell a man no, you have a good reason. Now, I want you to take a deep breath and close your eyes." Keri complied. "I'm going to kiss you again, and if you want me to stop, I will. I'm not going to take this very far, I promise."

A soft sigh left Keri's lips when Ryan's mouth covered hers in a kiss so gentle that she wanted to cry in pure wonder at a man acting so tenderly and caring with her. Her hands lifted, hesitated, then settled on Ryan's shoulders. Her fingertips pressed into the knit fabric of his shirt, then tensed.

"That's all right, love," he coaxed. "Feel free to touch me."

Ryan's brain raced. If he didn't know better, he'd almost think that Keri was a virgin—or one very frightened woman. He dreaded to think that her problem was the latter. He was sorely tempted to ask her who had hurt her so badly, but he didn't want her to withdraw again. Right now she was in his arms, and that was a huge step in the right direction.

"You wear a very distinctive perfume, Keri." It took a great effort to keep his voice level, not to mention his desire just to pick her up and carry her upstairs to bed. But he knew that with Keri he'd have to go slowly.

"I-it's"—she swallowed, unable to say more, since Ryan had again found her ear with the tip of his tongue and was carefully laving the curved surface—"it's Ruffles."

91

"Very feminine," he murmured, now nibbling his way around her earlobe.

Keri shivered when Ryan's tongue slid over the surface of her lips. She could taste cream mixed with chocolate icing from the doughnuts he had eaten. She sighed, allowing him access to the tart moisture of her mouth.

Ryan was hesitant about deepening their kiss. Instead of immediately accepting Keri's silent invitation, he concentrated on running his tongue over the smooth surface of her teeth and exploring her soft inner lip.

Keri felt the heat racing through her body. Deep down the fear threatened to surface, but each time it did, Ryan sensed her tension and worked again to relax her.

Keri discovered the muscles rippling along Ryan's back and the slightly rough skin of his neck, where his dark hair curled lovingly around her fingers. For what had seemed years she had thought that her emotions were dead. How wrong she had been. This simple kiss was swiftly turning into an exquisite torture she hadn't experienced before. Not even full lovemaking with Don had ever created the body-twisting feelings that Ryan could conjure up with just his mouth covering hers and his tongue discovering her taste.

For one wild moment Keri visualized their naked bodies entwined on the bed upstairs. She could see Ryan's body, slick with perspiration, poised over her, then their forms merging, she arching to meet his downward thrust, she losing control, she . . . he . . .

*"No!"* Keri gasped, breaking free. She stumbled off the couch and walked rapidly across the room, her arms wrapped around her body for protection.

Ryan lay back, breathing heavily. Keri had begun to respond to him until she had allowed her fear to take over. He wished he could meet the man who had hurt Keri so badly, because he'd like to turn the bastard into mincemeat.

"I'm sorry." Keri's pained whisper barely reached his ears.

"I said I'd stop if you wanted me to. I'm still in one piece," Ryan assured her. He rose to his feet and tucked his shirt back into his jeans. It was obvious that he was still heavily aroused.

"I—I didn't mean for it to go so far," Keri admitted. She was clearly ill at ease.

Ryan ran his fingers through his tousled hair. "I should let you rest."

She managed a weak smile. "I told you that we were more than an odd couple."

He pointed his forefinger at her, his thumb cocked upward to resemble a gun. "No arguments, lady." He walked to the front door with Keri following. Ryan opened the door and half turned toward her. One question had been nagging him for some time now, and he finally found the courage to ask it.

"Keri, are you acting as a surrogate mother for someone?"

Whatever Keri might have been expecting, this wasn't it. She resisted the urge to laugh. "No, Ryan, I'm not," she said softly. "Good night."

Surprisingly, Keri slept well that night. The next morning, she had plenty of energy to clean her house thoroughly and do two loads of laundry.

The afternoon was spent with conditioner slathered on her hair, a mud pack patted on her face, and cream applied to her feet, which were then thrust into heavy socks.

93

An oversize faded baseball jersey and cutoffs completed her unfashionable attire.

She groaned when the doorbell rang. What if it were Ryan? She could never let him see her like this!

"Keri, I know you're home," Amanda called out.

*This is even worse!* Keri thought as she headed for the door.

Amanda, immaculate as always, in navy linen pants and a cream silk shirt, stood in the doorway. "I gather you weren't expecting company." She swept past Keri. "I hope you haven't had that mud pack on too long. You wouldn't want your skin to turn into leather. It *is* made from organic materials, isn't it?"

"I don't remember," Keri murmured, pulling the towel from her hair and allowing straggly strands to drop to her shoulders. "There's iced tea in the refrigerator. I'll just wash this out." She retreated up the stairs.

Keri quickly showered off the hair conditioner and mud pack and returned downstairs.

"When was the last time you cleaned out your refrigerator?" Amanda walked out of the kitchen carrying two glasses, one filled with milk. "I hope that bottle of calcium tablets on the counter is new, rather than that you forget to take them."

"I've always hated milk," Keri said, irritated.

"Then you'll drink it all that much faster, won't you?" Amanda walked around the living room and stuck her finger in the flowerpots. "The earth is pretty dry. When was the last time this philodendron was watered?"

"Amanda, I know you haven't come here to check on my calcium pills or ask if I've watered my plants lately." Keri sipped the dreaded beverage under her sister's watchful eyes.

Ignoring Keri's question, she asked, "Has your nausea subsided?"

"With the help of medication, yes." Keri set the glass down on a nearby table.

"You've been entertaining, too, I see." Amanda held up a handkerchief. "Funny how the monogram matches Ryan Kincaid's initials." A ghost of a smile hovered on her lips. "Why don't you bring him out for dinner tomorrow?" She picked up the glass of milk and handed it back to Keri.

Keri shook her head. "Oh, no, you've vetoed every man I've ever dated. The only difference with Ryan is that I'm not dating or having an affair with him."

Amanda smiled, appearing very satisfied with Keri's answer. "You look like the Keri I remember," she mused. "He's bringing you back to life again."

Keri spun around in a complete circle. "I don't believe this!" she almost shouted. "Amanda, I can't have a man in my life and you know it! If anything, he feels pity for me." Even though she said it, she still hoped that it wasn't the case.

Amanda finished her glass of iced tea, walked into the kitchen, rinsed out the glass, and placed it in the dishwasher. "Why don't you come around one? I'll have Cal put steaks on the barbecue," she said. "And don't forget to finish your milk," she added as she left.

"We won't be there," Keri called after her.

"See you tomorrow, dear."

"I will not allow her to order me around," Keri muttered to herself. She picked up her glass of milk, swallowed its contents, and took the glass into the kitchen. "I will not ask Ryan to go, and I won't go either. I'm not ten years old anymore." She picked up the phone. "She can't order me around." She dialed a number. "I don't have to do something just because she tells me to." She listened to the phone on the other end of the line ring twice. "I'm an adult." A third ring then the sound of the line being picked up.

"Hello."

"Hello, Ryan. This is Keri."

"I'm flattered that you're calling me." Keri could picture his grin on the other end.

"Actually my sister would like you to come to dinner at her house tomorrow afternoon. Please don't feel bad if you have other plans," she urged him. "I've heard that cholera is sweeping the city."

Ryan chuckled. "I gather this is a command performance."

"That's a good word for it."

Ryan sat on his bed and looked out over the golf course. He doubted that Keri would have called him if it hadn't been for her sister's invitation. Was the woman that formidable? If any other woman had talked to him about a family dinner, he would have refused graciously without a second thought.

"What time shall I pick you up?" he asked politely. The sigh on the other end gave him the idea that Keri had hoped he wouldn't accept.

"Twelve-thirty," Keri told him. "Don't worry, you can leave your white tie and tails at home."

This time Ryan's chuckle turned into a full-bodied laugh. "Are you that frightened of her, Keri?"

"Terrified," she told him, then hung up.

Keri hadn't been entirely truthful. She wasn't terrified of Amanda. Yes, there were times when she felt intimidated by her older sister, but she also loved her dearly.

During their parents' many arguments and their neglect of their two daughters before they finally divorced, it had been Amanda who dried Keri's frightened tears, Amanda who had made sure Keri had clean clothes for school and saw to it that Keri finished her homework. Amanda had been the mother figure that young Keri needed even when their newly divorced mother was too busy trying to find a new husband.

There was only one time when Keri had refused to listen to her older sister. The result was a bad marriage. Keri was grateful that Amanda never said "I told you so" but silently offered her emotional support.

Keri might tease Amanda about her take-charge attitude toward her husband and sons, but she also saw the deep love the family shared, and she knew that counted a great deal more.


On Sunday morning Keri looked her wardrobe over carefully. She knew it was probably too soon to tell, but she could swear her waist had lost some of its slimness.

She chose a rose-colored cotton sleeveless sun dress that was held together by a discreetly placed button on the side. She fastened a silver chain around her neck and hunted up her bone-colored leather low-heeled sandals and slipped them on. Realizing her time was growing short, she French-braided her hair down her back with a dark rose ribbon threaded through the braid.

"Very nice," Ryan pronounced when he appeared at Keri's front door. "Do I pass inspection?" He turned slowly in a model's pose.

"I think you'll do," she said in a mock haughty tone.

Oh, yes, in sharply creased designer jeans and a melon-colored polo shirt, Ryan was the answer to a woman's prayers.

"I'm sorry to get you into this," she apologized once she was settled in the passenger seat of the Porsche. "I'm afraid that my sister can be a bit overpowering."

"You love her a great deal, don't you?"

"Yes, I do." Keri then remained silent except for giving Ryan directions.

Cal opened the front door and enveloped his sister-in-law in a bear hug.

"You're looking sexier every day," he teased Keri, then turned to Ryan. "Cal York, Mr. Kincaid. I've heard a lot of good things about you from many of your business associates."

Ryan cast a sly sidelong glance in Keri's direction. Hadn't she said something too? "Really?"

"I'm sorry to prick your balloon, but I never discuss my clients with anyone," she said sweetly.

"Come on in back," Cal urged, leading the way through a high-ceilinged living room with dark Spanish-style furniture. "How about a beer?" he asked Ryan.

"Sounds fine."

"I gather this means you'll start the barbecue." Amanda walked out of the kitchen with her hand out-stretched toward Ryan. "Hello, Ryan. I'm sure you don't mind if I call you that, do you? I'm glad you could come today. Our boys are out in the pool. Why don't you men go out back while Keri and I finish preparing the rest of the meal."

"I get the message." Cal smiled affectionately at his wife and winked at Ryan. "In case you haven't guessed," he said to Ryan, "we have just been dismissed. Why don't you go on out and I'll get the beers before I'm permanently banned from the kitchen?"

Ten minutes later Keri could hear the men talking together as if they had known each other for years. She kept glancing toward Amanda as she tore lettuce leaves apart for a tossed salad.

"What's your first impression?" Keri asked her finally.

"Very favorable." Amanda reached inside the refrigerator for the carrots. "He wants you, Keri. And not just for a business relationship."

Keri inhaled sharply through her nose and blew out through her mouth. "It can't be, Amanda, and you know it. The trouble is, he's much too stubborn to acknowledge it."

"Have you told him . . . everything?"

Keri's lips tightened. She knew that Amanda was asking if Keri had mentioned to Ryan the identity of the baby's father. That had been Keri's secret from the beginning; she hadn't ever told her sister that Larry was the father, although Amanda had guessed it from the beginning. She shook her head in a no-nonsense reply. A laugh minus the mirth left her lips. "He asked me if I was a surrogate mother."

Amanda studied Keri with her ultracritical eye. "Your color still doesn't look good. Have you seen the doctor recently."

Keri nodded. " 'The first trimester is always the worst,' " she quoted Dr. Chalmers.

"Nonsense!" Amanda scoffed. "I wasn't sick a day when I carried the boys. I think you should see another doctor."

"You and Ryan both." She smiled wryly.

99

The steaks and baked potatoes had been cooked perfectly. During the meal Keri quietly observed as Amanda interrogated Ryan with consummate skill. It wasn't long before the older woman knew just about everything about Ryan except for his blood type.

"Are you sure Cal's the attorney in the family?" he whispered to Keri when they had a moment alone.

She smiled mischievously. "I think Amanda taught Cal everything he knows."

After dinner Keri relaxed on a chaise longue on the patio. She couldn't understand why she felt so tired when her day had been spent quietly. Both Ryan and Amanda noticed the weary set of Keri's features.

"I hate to break up the evening, but I have an early day tomorrow," Ryan announced, standing up and looking toward a drooping Keri. He held out a helping hand and pulled her to her feet.

Amanda shot Ryan a silent look of gratitude. They both knew that a direct reference to Keri's fatigue would only receive a protest from her.

"Thanks for a wonderful dinner," Ryan said sincerely when Amanda and Cal had walked them outside.

"You must come back again," Amanda told him.

Ryan smiled. "Does this mean I passed the test?"

Amanda's smile didn't quite reach her eyes. "I won't see her hurt."

"Amanda . . ." Keri's voice carried a hidden warning.

"Yes, dear." She was unperturbed. "You be sure to get all your rest. I'll talk to you next week."

Keri almost collapsed in the car seat. She laid her head back and released a sigh.

"Tired?" Ryan pressed her hand briefly.

"Umm." She nodded. "And this will be a hectic week because I ran a lot of ads and one consultant is out on vacation."

"Why the ads? I thought your agency only catered to temporary positions."

"Advertising gets us many of our applicants. We also have some long-term temporary jobs that we need people to fill," Keri explained. "I advertise in every Sunday-morning edition. Monday and Tuesday are usually the busiest days of the week for us. Lately, I come home feeling ready to drop."

Ryan frowned. "You take too much on. You're going to need to rest more or you'll be flat on your back in bed for several months," he warned.

"I watch myself," Keri protested tersely.

"The way you did when you battled those bouts of nausea?"

Keri grimaced. She always hated being reminded when she was in the wrong.

When they arrived at Keri's house, Ryan walked her to her door. "I still want you to call another doctor," he urged, pulling a small case out of his jeans pocket and extracting a white business card from a leather folder. "Please, Keri."

She accepted the card. How could she refuse him when he asked so sweetly?

"Good night, Ryan." Her hand rested on the doorknob and she was ready to escape inside. She knew she didn't dare risk a repeat of the night before.

Ryan gently pried her fingers loose from the doorknob and lifted her hand. He placed a soft kiss in the center of her palm and carefully curled her fingers over the tingling center.

"Now that I know your sister approves of me, I'll be sure to keep in touch," he murmured. "Sweet dreams."

Keri watched Ryan leave, then went inside. Her mind whirled over the events of the day.

It wasn't until she got ready for bed that she remembered the business card he had given her. Keri found it lying on the dresser, where she had placed it along with her jewelry.

The address wasn't far from her office; she recognized it as being that of a fairly large medical center. She shouldn't have been surprised by the name, either.

"Wouldn't you know it would be a woman," she grumbled, tossing the card back onto the dresser. Right now, all she cared about was getting many blissful hours of sleep.

## CHAPTER SIX

Dr. Joyce Reynolds turned out to be the kind of woman Keri could imagine as a "friend" of Ryan's. She was in her mid- to late thirties and had deep auburn hair coiled in a chignon at her nape; her patient-oriented manner seemed guaranteed to calm the most hysterical mother-to-be.

"Actually, I'm surprised that I would get a patient referral from Ryan." Joyce smiled warmly. For a moment she wondered if Ryan was the father but instantly dismissed that thought. She doubted this woman had ever been intimately involved with Ryan. So how had they met each other?

"Mr. Kincaid is one of my clients and knew that I was having trouble with my regular OB," Keri said quietly. "He suggested I see you."

Joyce's bright blue eyes sparkled with amusement. "Meaning he called and made the appointment?" She chuckled. "I think he has some bulldozer in him."

Keri shifted uncomfortably. Just how well did Ryan and this woman know each other?

"My husband and Ryan were fraternity brothers," Joyce explained. "To this day I can't understand how the college remained standing after some of their so-called pranks."

"It must have been difficult for you to go through medical school and keep up a marriage too," Keri speculated.

"It wasn't easy, but Jay was just the support I needed." Joyce folded her hands and placed them on her desk. "You're not going to like what I'm going to say." She paused. "Of course, nothing is official until I get the lab results and your paperwork from Dr. Chalmers's office, but my instincts are usually pretty correct."

"Why do I get the feeling that you're not going to tell me that I'm expecting twins?" Keri surmised wryly.

Dr. Reynolds smiled and shook her head. "I only wish that could be true."

Alarm flashed over Keri's face. "Is the baby—?"

Joyce hastened to soothe her fear. "The fetus is fine. The one I'm worried about is you. Your skin tone isn't good, you've already admitted that you tire very easily, you have high blood pressure and had a bad time with almost constant nausea until something was prescribed for you. I'd even hazard a guess that you're anemic. You're going to have to slow down, Keri, or be warned that you could lose your child."

Keri looked down at her clenched hands held rigidly in her lap. "None of this is deliberate," she whispered painfully. "I take my vitamins, I exercise, I do all that I'm supposed to."

Joyce's smile was faintly sad. "No matter how good you are, Keri, sometimes Mother Nature has different ideas. If you decide to continue under my care, I'll want you in here every week so I can monitor your blood pressure. I also would like to prescribe a different medication for your nausea, since you said that the one you're taking makes you drowsy."

Keri nodded, ready to agree to anything.

"There's one other thing," Joyce added sternly. "If I decide you'll need complete bed rest toward the end of your pregnancy, I'll expect you to obey my orders without any argument. Understand?"

Keri nodded meekly.

Joyce's stern demeanor relaxed. "I'll do what I can to give you a healthy baby, Keri. All I ask is that you cooperate. Start leaving work an hour or so early and take a short nap when you get home. Always keep a few soda crackers in your purse for your nausea, and mainly, just start relaxing. A pregnancy isn't meant to be frightening."

"Just awe-inspiring." Keri managed a weak smile.

Joyce scribbled on a prescription pad, tore the sheet off, and handed it to Keri.

"I'll see you in a week, then." She stood up and held out her hand.

Keri stopped at the reception desk to pay her bill and schedule her next appointment.

"Well?" Serena demanded the moment Keri walked through the office door.

"Just fine." Well, it wasn't entirely a lie.

Barb cornered Keri before she could sit down. "What did the doctor say?"

Keri laughed as she dropped into her chair. "Perhaps I should just make an announcement: The doctor said everything is fine."

Barb looked skeptical upon hearing Keri's breezy statement. "I'm sure that she told you to take it easy," she guessed. "And don't try to tell me any differently, Keri Burke."

"Barb, I'm sleeping ten to twelve hours a night now.

Pretty soon I won't have any time to work," Keri objected.

"Would that be so bad?" Barb countered. "Keri, the agency is doing great. No offense, but if we had to do without you for a few months, we could. There is such a thing as a phone if a major problem crops up."

"Well . . ." Keri pretended to deliberate. She picked up the telephone message slips and sorted them according to degree of importance. "Perhaps I will begin leaving earlier in the afternoon."

"Sure, if we throw you out bodily," Barb taunted.

Keri wasn't surprised to find five messages from Ryan, all insisting that she call him the minute she arrived at the office. The others were from various clients and several applicants.

"Barb, Mr. Carey from Timmons Electric is on line four for you," Serena called out.

Barb nodded. "I wonder what his complaints are this time." She left the office and headed for her desk.

Keri informed Serena that she wasn't taking calls for a while and proceeded to work her way through her messages. Ryan's were put at the bottom of the pile. She already knew why he had been calling.

Keri had never had a man show such genuine interest in her life or health. All Don had ever cared about was that his clothes had been sent to the cleaners and he had a hot meal when he came home from work. If Keri had so much as a cold, he left her strictly alone because he was afraid of catching her germs.

But even though Ryan seemed concerned about her, Keri had read Ryan's personality from their first meeting. If he wanted what he saw, he took it. And for some unknown reason he wanted Keri.

"In a few months I'll resemble a hippopotamus. You'd think he liked fat women," she muttered to herself. But Keri had seen the dark gleam in Ryan's eyes when he looked at her, and knew that no matter how fat she got during her pregnancy, he would still view her as a desirable woman.

Involuntarily, Keri recalled the taste of Ryan's mouth the night he had kissed her so very thoroughly. At the same time she couldn't forget the bitter twinge of fear warring with her sensual nature. Ryan was a man whose physical nature could carry a woman to heaven, but perhaps to hell also.

Keri shuddered. The fear was threatening to overtake her again. She swiftly shook her head to banish her conflicting thoughts. She wanted Ryan out of her life! Or did she?

She was plowing doggedly through her paperwork when the intercom buzzer sounded.

"Yes?"

"Keri, I've held Mr. Kincaid off for the past half hour. Will you please talk to him before he tears my throat out over the phone?" Serena pleaded. "I swear, he sounds angrier each time he calls."

Keri sighed. She had a pretty good idea how Ryan acted over the phone, and it wasn't fair to subject Serena to his deadly brand of intimidation.

"All right, I'll speak to him."

"He's on line two."

Nevertheless, Keri allowed the tiny phone light to blink another moment before she punched the button.

"Good afternoon," she greeted him in an even voice.

The silence was almost terrifying, although she knew he'd never do anything to hurt her.

"Your receptionist said that you've been in your office for the past hour and a half." He enunciated each word with a cold tone. "I specifically requested that you call me as soon as you got in."

*"Requested?"* Keri asked archly. *"Demanded* is probably more like it."

Silence.

"One more thing: Don't you ever try your cold intimidation tactics on Serena again. I won't have her upset because of you." Keri was now warming up to her subject. "I have many clients and other more important problems to deal with than giving you the blow-by-blow account of my doctor's visit that I know you'll demand."

This time the silence felt even darker.

"Are you finished?" Ryan finally asked in a chilling tone.

"No!" she declared defiantly. "I just can't think of what else I had to tell you."

"You never thought that perhaps I was calling for business reasons, did you?" he said frostily.

Keri could feel a headache coming on. "What's wrong? Did Cassie stay too many steps ahead of you?"

Ryan's sharply exhaled breath sounded loud in her ear. "When you find the time, I would appreciate you calling a Doris Phelps. She's the personnel director for Landers Computers and needs four secretaries and six clerks to set up a temporary office until the company moves out here in six months."

Keri gulped. Six months! Talk about the temp order of a lifetime!

"A new client of yours?" she asked.

"Do you want her number or not?" Ryan barked.

108

"Yes, I would, Mr. Kincaid," she snapped back. "Thank you."

He gave her the number and repeated the name of the person she was to contact.

Ryan's voice softened. "Keri, I know you're an independent lady, but I was concerned about your doctor's appointment. I do care about you, you stubborn little witch," he added humorously.

"Everything was fine, Ryan," she reassured him. "I have to go. Thank you for the recommendation." It wasn't until she hung up that she realized that he hadn't mentioned meeting during or after working hours.

Keri called Doris Matthews and soon discovered that Ryan had laid the groundwork for her. The woman had already heard of K.B. Temps' excellent reputation and was more than willing to talk to Keri about her personnel needs, so they arranged to discuss it during a breakfast meeting two days from then.

An hour later Keri felt as if she had run a marathon. Remembering Dr. Reynolds's admonition, she dumped the last of her paperwork into her briefcase and quickly cleared her desk. "I'll be home if you need me," she told Serena on her way out of the office.

Keri never realized how good coming home could feel. She undressed and pulled a cotton caftan over her naked body and was just preparing to lie down on the bed when the doorbell rang.

"Give me a break," she moaned aloud, walking down the stairs.

Max stood at the door, holding a large bouquet of flowers arranged in a clear glass pot.

"These were left for you, lass," he said gruffly.

"How lovely," Keri said, sighing and reaching out for the colorful bouquet. "Come in, Max," she invited him.

The elderly man shook his head. "My poker night," he explained. "You're home early."

"If the boss can't take off early, who can?" she quipped. "Thank you for bringing them over, Max."

After he left, Keri carried her flowers into the living room. She didn't have to read the attached card to learn the identity of the sender. She already knew his name.

*These aren't an apology,* the card said. There was no signature.

*So he won't apologize if he can absolutely help it, will he?* Keri thought, setting the vase in the middle of the coffee table.

Keri didn't find it difficult to lie down and take a short nap. In fact, she only had to stretch out on the bed and close her eyes in order to drift off. After her nap she fixed herself a light dinner and settled down in the living room with her paperwork.

Keri compared the monthly reports for that year and was pleased to find that the figures steadily increased. She knew the time had definitely arrived for her to advertise for another consultant—maybe even look for additional office space. Something on the other side of town, perhaps.


Keri met with Doris Matthews two days later and found a warm-natured woman in her fifties who could be hardheaded when necessary.

Keri wrote out the various job descriptions and promised Doris her new secretarial and clerical help first thing Monday morning.

There had been no word from Ryan.

Several times Keri picked up the telephone and began to dial Ryan's number, then just as quickly replaced the receiver. Calling him would be the same as saying she felt dependent on him, and she couldn't do that.

On Friday afternoon Keri was going over the weekly billing when she received an unexpected visitor.

"You look tired."

She looked up and faced her caller. "Your compliments are still overwhelming." She watched Ryan fold himself into a chair.

Ryan smiled and shook his head. Whether it was frustration at her or with himself was unclear. "You always throw it back tenfold, Keri." He cocked his head to one side. "Doris said that the two of you had a good meeting."

"She's impressed with the people I've sent her," Keri murmured.

"Who wouldn't be?" Ryan replied, studying her. He didn't like the pale shadows under her eyes and the fragile cast of her skin. He had tried quizzing Joyce about Keri's health, but the doctor wasn't forthcoming with information. "You know very well I can't and *won't* discuss Keri with you," Joyce had snapped when Ryan had tried to question her. "You're not even a relative. To be blunt, her health is none of your business. She'll have to be the one to tell you."

Looking at Keri's quiet features, Ryan knew that she wouldn't tell him anything. She would rather go it alone than accept his help. He was going to continue to bide his time. The day would come when Keri would need him, and he intended to be there.

Not wanting to be the focus of Ryan's merciless gaze

any longer, Keri swung her chair around and looked out the window. She watched men and women standing at the corner, waiting for the light to change. She studied one woman in particular who held the hand of a small boy four or five years of age. A strong twisting sensation knotted Keri's insides. Would her child have that perpetual smile, that look of enchantment with the world?

*Oh, God!* she cried in silent prayer for a healthy child. Then her attention was sharply diverted in another direction.

*No! It can't be! He's in Canada!* Keri almost felt the urge to scream. There were lots of men with reddish brown hair who walked with an arrogant swagger. Her fingers tightened on the arms of the chair.

"Keri?" Ryan asked, watching her face turn from pale to white.

She heard nothing. She was too busy staring at the man striding down the sidewalk across the street.

Ryan's voice sharpened: "Keri!"

She slowly returned to the present. She turned her chair back around. "I'm very busy, Ryan," Keri said stiffly, refusing to meet his eyes.

"Actually, I came by to see if you'd go out to dinner with Lacy and me tonight," he explained, wondering what had caused her distress.

She shook her head. "That's your night with your daughter," she protested.

"Lacy made the suggestion," Ryan informed her. He frowned, noticing that the color hadn't returned to Keri's cheeks. "Keri, are you all right?"

"I'm fine," she managed to reply. If she turned around and looked out the window, would she still see him? "Please, Ryan, I have to finish this before I leave."

He was tempted to ignore her less-than-subtle hint. "I'll see you later, then."

"Yes," Keri said, not realizing what she had said. "Have a good evening with your daughter."

The moment she was alone again, she swung the chair back around and scanned the street with searching eyes. Only now the man was gone.

"It can't be," Keri whispered her painful chant. "It can't be." It was a long time before she returned to her paperwork.

It was a cold and numb Keri who walked into her house an hour later. She entered her bedroom and undressed, dropping her clothes onto the carpet. She put on jeans and a pale green long-sleeved pullover sweater. The inner cold was slowly reaching outward to envelop her entire body.

Keri suddenly collapsed onto the bed. Her body shook with violent tremors. She remained there for well over an hour until she was able to rouse herself to go downstairs and fix herself a cup of hot tea; she needed something to warm the chill in her blood. She took a pill to ease the rapidly rising nausea, and left the room.

Her shaking hands were just lifting the cup to her lips when her doorbell pealed.

*"No!"* The cup shattered on the floor and hot tea splashed on her bare feet.

"Keri?" a young female voice called out. "Are you okay?"

Keri cursed under her breath and carefully stepped over the broken crockery. "Coming!"

Keri pulled the front door open and found Lacy on the other side.

"Hi," Lacy greeted her with an uncertain smile. "I hope I'm not intruding. I thought I heard a crash."

"I'm the original butterfingers." Keri was still working on slowing her heart rate. "Why don't you come in while I clean up the mess? Would you like something to drink?"

Lacy shook her head as she followed Keri into the kitchen. "Let me do it, Keri," she offered. "You could cut your foot."

In no time the mess was cleared and they were seated in the living room, Keri silently wondering why Lacy had come, Lacy questioning the frightened look on Keri's face.

"Dad said that you weren't feeling well and wouldn't be able to go out with us tonight." Lacy smiled, the action lighting dark eyes so like her father's. "It's because of my father, isn't it?" Her smile turned a bit more impish at the rueful expression on Keri's face. "I think you frighten him."

At this, Keri laughed. "Frighten him? I'm sorry, Lacy, but I doubt anyone or anything frightens Ryan."

"You do." She affirmed her pronouncement with a knowledge beyond her years. "Every woman I've ever seen around Dad falls over backward to do his bidding. They hang on to his every word as if it were gold." She stopped abruptly and flushed, realizing it sounded strange for a daughter to be discussing her father's social life.

"Don't worry, it's safe," Keri assured the young girl with a smile. "I never liked being part of a crowd."

"That's it exactly!" Lacy agreed excitedly. "Dad— well, he likes to take care of people, to feel in charge, and you don't let him take over. Please don't be mad at him. He does mean well."

Keri chuckled at Lacy's statement. "Yes, he does," she agreed softly.

"Do you think you could change your mind about tonight?" Lacy asked hopefully.

Keri shook her head. "I can't explain it all to you, Lacy, and as a result, your father can't understand, either. I'm just better off on my own." She had taken her nausea medication, so why was her stomach still acting upset?

Lacy shrugged. "Dad didn't send me here. I just thought, well, you seem so nice." She added brightly: "We go out for brunch Sunday mornings. Will you go with us then?"

"I think you'd better ask your father first," Keri teased.

"No problem there," Lacy declared airily, jumping to her feet. "We'll pick you up at eleven. Thanks, Keri." She flashed a bright smile and then left.

Keri regretted her decision once Lacy was gone. She made herself another cup of tea, but it disagreed with her, as did the slice of toast she had fixed. In the end she went to bed early that evening and slept until late morning.

Saturday was spent doing light housecleaning until a queasy stomach and a backache took precedence.

"I don't need to get the flu now," Keri complained to her reflection in the bathroom mirror on Saturday night. Ryan had called earlier to confirm brunch the next morning. Keri told him she would be ready.

On Sunday morning Keri knew she wasn't going anywhere. The nausea was much greater than before; she couldn't even keep water down. She tried calling Ryan's house but there was no answer. When her stomach felt more stable, she dressed in jogging pants and a loose shirt.

"He *would* be early," she groaned at the knock at her door. "Oh, well, he'll definitely see that I'm not making up an excuse." She threw open the door and froze at the sight of her visitor.

"Hello, Keri." A tall man with dark auburn hair greeted her with a careless grin. "Look who just flew in from Canada."

Keri held on to the door for support for fear her legs would buckle under her.

"Larry"—she said the name under her breath as if it were a dreaded curse.

# CHAPTER SEVEN

"Aren't you going to invite me in?" Larry's voice was that of a man sure of his welcome.

"I don't think so." Keri's tone was icy, while her eyes shot darts straight into his heart.

"Oh, come on, love. After all, we've meant a great deal to each other." He leered at her and slid into the entry-way.

Keri's entire body was one mass of tightened nerves. "Get out of here, Larry," she ordered. "We have nothing to say to each other."

His eyes swept upward to the second floor, then back over her disheveled figure. "Oh, I get it: You've got company. Hey, baby, I'm flexible." He uttered a dirty laugh.

Keri inhaled sharply. "You bastard." Her voice shook with barely suppressed fury and a deep fear of the man standing before her. *"Get out!"*

Larry wandered around the living room. "Nothing's changed, I see. Of course, it's only been, what, three, three and a half months?"

"I have friends coming over and I want you out of here." Keri could feel the last thread of composure steadily slipping away.

"Male friends?" he asked suggestively. Why hadn't she seen this side of him before? Larry stopped at the coffee table and glanced at several colorful brochures lying on the waxed surface. "Hm, what are these?" he asked as he picked one up.

*"No!"* Keri leaped at him, but his hand shackling her wrists kept her fingers from scratching his face.

" 'Prenatal Care' . . . 'A Healthy Pregnancy' . . ." Larry stopped reading and looked at her face, which was now pale with horror. "It's my baby, isn't it?" Larry asked hoarsely.

"No!" Keri denied vehemently. "There's someone else."

He released her hands, stood back, and laughed. "Hey, Keri, I'm not that stupid. You're having my kid."

By now the tears were flowing freely down Keri's cheeks and the nausea was returning.

"Just get out of here, Larry, or I'll call the police."

He shook his head. His handsome features twisted into a leer again. "You're a prominent businesswoman, lover. You don't want any scandal. So, when do I become a father officially?"

Keri sobbed. She felt as if she were losing her meager hold on reality. She couldn't speak.

"You don't."

Keri was shocked to hear him. She spun around and looked at Ryan with shimmering eyes filled with gratitude. His timing was perfect!

He stood in the doorway, dressed in black slacks and a charcoal-and-white-striped shirt. There was an air of dark menace about him as he gazed at a now discomfited Larry. Ryan's eyes held a devil's gleam.

"Hey, I don't know who you are, but we're having a private conversation here," Larry blustered under Ryan's compelling gaze. "You'll have to wait your turn."

118

Ryan's hands clenched at his sides, and the muscle twitching in his cheek betrayed how badly he wanted to take this man apart. "You have no business here," he said harshly.

"Sure I do. She's having my kid," Larry replied, withering at Ryan's expression of disgust.

Keri stood off to the side, afraid to speak. She had never seen Ryan in such a dangerous mood, and she prayed that his temper would never be directed toward her. She wrapped her arms around her body for self-protection.

"The baby is mine," Ryan said in the sternest voice Keri had ever heard. "Now, get out."

Larry turned to Keri, still unaware of how to respond to the sense of danger emanating from the man standing across the room. "You were a busy lady back then."

With a roar Ryan pounced on the other man.

*"No!"* Keri screamed, stepping back and almost colliding with a chair.

In the space of a moment Larry was lying on the floor, using a handkerchief to staunch the flow of blood from his nose as Ryan stood back.

"I don't ever want to see you near her again, you son of a bitch," Ryan ground out, "or so help me, the next time I'll kill you. And that's definitely a promise."

Larry stumbled to his feet and staggered to the open door. "She's not worth it," he mumbled defiantly. "She's nothing but a block of ice." He ran out the door before Ryan could inflict further damage.

Ryan turned to Keri. "Are you all right?" he asked softly, holding out his arms to fold her against himself.

Keri could see traces of blood on his bruised knuckles,

which only added to her distress. "Please go away," she begged, still crying deeply.

"Keri, you have to calm yourself," he urged her quietly.

*"Calm?"* she almost shouted. "How can I be calm after what just happened here?"

Ryan drew a deep breath. Handling a hysterical woman was definitely out of his realm of expertise. He was tempted to ask Lacy to come in. Perhaps she could soothe Keri. He headed for the front door, only to be stopped by a heart-stopping scream and the sound of his name. He spun back to Keri.

"Ryan, I'm bleeding!" she gasped as a sharp pain sliced through her midsection. She doubled over in agony.

He saw the spots of blood on her cotton pants and wasted no time. *"Lacy!"* he roared, and the young girl was standing in the doorway a moment later. Her terrified eyes took in Ryan steering Keri to the couch. "Go upstairs and find a blanket," he ordered. He softened his harsh tone when he looked back at Keri. "I'm going to call Joyce, Keri. I'll be right back."

"No!" Her eyes were wild with fear. "It's too late, Ryan."

He shook his head. "We don't know that. Let me call Joyce and I'll come right back," he promised.

Ryan used the kitchen phone, silently grateful that he didn't have to go through an answering service but could reach the doctor at her home. In a few moments he had explained the situation to Joyce.

"I'll meet you at the hospital," she told him, wasting no time on the phone.

And neither did Ryan. He found Lacy wrapping a pale

blue blanket around a shaking Keri and talking softly to keep her calm.

"Here's your chance." Ryan extracted his keys from his slacks pocket and tossed them to Lacy. He was glad he had driven the Audi that day. Keri would be more comfortable in the backseat. He leaned over and gently picked her up, cradling her in his arms. "Lacy, you're going to drive us to the hospital."

Lacy's eyes widened. "I only got my permit a week ago," she exclaimed, gulping.

Ryan looked down at Keri, who clutched him tightly around the neck. He looked back at his daughter. "Grab Keri's purse," he commanded over his shoulder as he headed for the door.

Lacy ran ahead and opened the rear door of the dark-blue Audi. Ryan placed Keri inside as carefully as he could, then got in after her. Soon the car was speeding down the street with a grim-faced Ryan giving directions to Lacy.

"Don't let me die, Ryan," Keri begged tearfully. Her face was buried against his shoulder, and in years to come her memories of those moments would be of the sharp tang of his after-shave blending with the warm scent of his skin and the soothing sound of his voice in her ear. "Please don't let me die."

"You're not going to die, Keri," Ryan vowed fiercely. "No one is going to take you away from me. *No one.*" There was a stinging dampness in his eyes. At that moment he would have fought the Devil himself to keep Keri with him. He pressed a hungry kiss against her temple and continued murmuring in her ear. The words didn't always make sense, but they did comfort her.

"Park at the emergency entrance," he directed when the hospital appeared in sight.

Lacy slowed the car and turned into the wide driveway. When she stopped, she jumped out of the car and ran around to the back door.

A white-uniformed attendant appeared with a gurney. "You Kincaid?"

"Yeah." Ryan carefully placed Keri on the cushioned surface.

"Don't leave me," Keri pleaded, grabbing hold of his hand.

His smile was meant to reassure her, and it did. "I won't." He could see Joyce hurrying down the hall.

"Room B," she called out to the attendant. "The waiting room is to your left, Ryan."

"No!" Keri gripped his hand tighter.

He silently pleaded with the doctor, who nodded.

"After you've parked the car, wait out here," he told Lacy.

Keri cried out as the pain intensified. She had remained quiet during the car ride, but with the fire spreading through her abdomen, she couldn't remain silent any longer.

Ryan continued to hold Keri's hand and speak softly as Joyce swiftly examined her. The doctor murmured something to the nurse, who then prepared an IV and efficiently slid the needle into Keri's arm. She was also given an injection.

In a matter of seconds Keri was asleep. Ryan looked questioningly at Joyce.

"You may as well wait outside," she advised him quietly. "I'll need to perform a D & C."

Ryan paled, understanding the significance. "Will she be all right?"

Joyce nodded. "I'll be out to talk to you later."

Ryan looked down at Keri, whose strained features had now relaxed.

"The father was there when I arrived and she was pretty upset," he explained. "Did the shock cause the miscarriage?"

"Out," Joyce ordered. "And no, but it probably didn't help her any."

Ryan walked slowly down the hall to the waiting room. Lacy was curled up in the corner of a vinyl couch. She jumped to her feet when her father appeared.

"Is she all right?" she asked breathlessly.

"She lost the baby." He sighed, sitting on the couch. He placed his hand on the back of his neck and tried to rub the tension away. Funny how slowly the past few minutes had gone by.

"Dad?" Lacy ventured quietly, putting her hand on his arm. "I read somewhere that it's just nature's way of protecting the mother's health."

Ryan let out a strangled sound. He pulled his daughter to him.

"Oh, God," he murmured, resting his cheek against the top of her head. "I must have done something right at one time in my life to deserve you."

"Dad?" Lacy whispered. "Will you hold that thought when you see the scratch on the passenger side of the car? I kinda misjudged a post. Don't worry, I'll pay to have it fixed."

Ryan dropped a kiss in her hair. "We'll talk about it later."

123

By the time Joyce finally came out to talk to Ryan, he was pacing the floor.

"She's all right and is in Recovery right now," Joyce told him. "But I will want to keep her here for a few days." She cast a glance toward Lacy, who was seated out of earshot. "This was definitely not a time for Keri to become pregnant."

"Meaning . . . ?"

"She's just too run-down. I've been afraid since the first time she came in to see me that she wouldn't carry this child to full term. It's just as well it happened now, though." Joyce looked at Ryan sharply. "She's too fragile for you, Ryan. And much too vulnerable. Keri is nothing like the other women you've dated."

His smile softened his angular features. "I know, and I think the one you should be worried about is me. When can I see her?"

"This evening. I'd like her to have plenty of time to wake up," Joyce said, not missing the relief in Ryan's eyes when he heard the verdict. Perhaps he was right. For once, Ryan could be the one in trouble with the opposite sex!

Keri slept for the rest of the day. When she awoke, the ache in the center of her body told her the final verdict before Joyce came in to see her.

"I'm sorry," Joyce said as she checked Keri's pulse, then sat in the chair next to the bed.

"It's best." Keri managed a weak smile. "You and I both know that."

Joyce jotted down the readings on Keri's chart. "Ryan said that the child's father was with you this morning." It didn't take a doctor to note Keri's sudden agitation. "Had he been invited there?" she asked casually.

"I . . . ah . . . I'm still very tired." Keri nervously pleated the sheet with her fingers and turned her head away.

Joyce knew better than to push at that moment. "If you experience any discomfort, just call the nurse." She stood up and slid her hands into the deep pockets of her lab coat. "And, Keri, if you want to talk, I'm willing to listen."

Keri still refused to look at Joyce. She didn't look up again until the door whispered shut.

On a table next to the window was a miniature garden in a large, shallow glass bowl, a gift from Ryan. Keri smiled: He had remembered her love of greenery.

She recalled his hoarsely whispered words of solace during the frantic drive to the hospital. While her body was racked with pain and fear of dying filled her thoughts, Ryan had been her lifeline to sanity. He had held and consoled her. He had constantly assured her that everything was all right, and not once had he allowed his own fears to creep into his voice.

Keri's eyes filled with tears. This man was so very, very special! How many men would befriend a pregnant woman, force her out of the shell into which she was withdrawing, and then remain with her during a traumatic time in her life? Yet, Ryan had done that and more.

She knew it was best that she had lost her baby, but she still mourned the tiny entity that had never had a chance to experience life. She was so lost in her thoughts that she was barely aware of a cool palm cupping her cheek.

"No more tears, Keri." The low voice washed over her like rough silk.

She shifted her position in the bed, wincing when a twinge of pain hit her.

Ryan quickly set a vase of roses on the night table. "Shall I call the nurse?" he asked with alarm.

"No," she said. "I'm just finding out that my body can't move as easily as it did before." She reached up to take his hand and turn it over to inspect the grazed skin. "And I thought things like that only happened in the movies." She raised her eyes to his. "You didn't have to."

"Yes I did." The back of his other hand stroked her cheek in a feather-light caress.

Funny, Keri had thought that she was over tears by then, but it wasn't true.

"Perhaps you should buy stock in a paper company," she said, sniffing as she accepted a tissue from Ryan. "How can you stand to be around someone who more or less resembles a rain cloud?"

Ryan's lips curved into a smile. "You haven't cried half as much as you think you have," he explained. He pulled up a chair and sat on the not-so-comfortable vinyl seat.

"Where's Lacy?" Keri asked.

"She's home. You have to be sixteen to visit in this wing, so she's fixing dinner for me." A grimace passed fleetingly over his face.

"You don't look very pleased."

"You wouldn't be, either. Lacy's flunked home economics twice. Her idea of a full-course meal is a hamburger, fries, and a hot-fudge sundae. The last time she cooked dinner for me, it took weeks to get the smell out of the kitchen."

Keri smiled. She couldn't help but hear the love in Ryan's voice when he talked about his daughter.

"I left a message with your answering service so your

office will know where you are. I also brought you some of your things." Ryan held up a cream-colored leather tote bag. "I hope I remembered everything. You may want to check; I can bring anything I've missed tomorrow." He set the bag on the bed next to Keri.

She flushed as she examined the contents. Oh, yes, Ryan hadn't forgotten anything, including underwear. He had chosen her prettiest nightgowns, a robe, and makeup. A couple of books from her bedside table had also been tossed in.

"If you tell me what kind of magazines you like to read, I'll pick some up for you," Ryan offered.

Keri shook her head. "You've done more than enough and I really thank you."

He picked up one of her hands and brought it to his lips. "It wasn't so bad, was it?" he teased lightly. "Having to rely on someone else?"

"It appears that I have no choice," she answered dryly.

Ryan held Keri's hand lightly clasped between his own. Her fingers grazed the sandpaper-rough surface of his chin.

"He was telling the truth, wasn't he? About being the father." His quiet, matter-of-fact voice disguised the gut-twisting tension in his body.

Keri tried to pull her hand away, but Ryan refused to relinquish his prize.

"I'm not going to let you continue hiding from me, Keri," Ryan insisted. "I allowed you to withdraw into your shell before because your emotions were so fragile. I won't allow it to continue, and I'm sure you know that your retreating days are over."

"Why?" she cried out, rolling onto her side and raising herself up on one elbow. "Why are you doing this?"

Ryan's eyes bored into hers. "Because I'm in love with you."

How those words haunted Keri all that night. Ryan had left soon after with the quiet promise to be in the next day. The kiss he had brushed over her lips still tingled.

She lay huddled under the covers, praying that Ryan hadn't spoken the truth. The trouble was, she knew that he had.

"He can't love me," she whispered to the silent room. "Because I have no love to give him and he's a man who should receive as much as he gives."

It wasn't until dawn that she finally drifted into an uneasy sleep.

Keri didn't lack visitors the next few days, as the women in her office took turns coming in to see her, and Max was by several times. Ryan also usually dropped by each morning and during the day. Fresh flowers arrived from him each morning, and Lacy even called her in the afternoons to moan over final exams and just to chat. Keri grew to look forward to the young girl's calls.

Amanda was at Keri's side that first evening and returned to the hospital each day. "I don't want to sound coldhearted, but I feel this was for the best," she told Keri during her first visit. "The circumstances—well . . ." Her eyes glistened with tears. "I'm just glad Ryan was there to take care of you."

"What is it about Ryan Kincaid that makes everyone think he should be my keeper?" Keri demanded, shifting uncomfortably in the bed. "I should think by now that I've more than adequately proved that I can take care of myself." She faltered under her sister's skeptical gaze. "Pretty much, that is."

"Did you ever stop to think about why your marriage to Don failed?" Amanda asked bluntly.

Keri nodded. "I did a lot of serious thinking when we first separated, and realized I had made a fairly common mistake: I married a man just like Dad. I, who vowed I wouldn't suffer through the same problems my mother had, walked right into an identical marriage."

"And what about Ryan Kincaid?" Amanda asked slyly.

"He's arrogant, bullying . . ." Keri knew she would run out of adjectives unless she started on *tender, gentle, caring, good-looking,* and so on.

"Yet, nothing like our father," Amanda pointed out smugly.

"Well, yes," she agreed reluctantly.

"He won't run very fast if you decide to catch him," she advised with a laugh at her sister's rueful expression.


"I'm sure you'll be pleased to hear that I'm releasing you in the morning," Joyce announced on Wednesday evening. "Of course, it's still going to be awhile before you'll be running in a marathon. Your body isn't meant to take on the long hours and abuse you've been heaping on it lately."

"It has to when you own a fairly new business and want to keep it out of the red," Keri countered, then sighed. "And I paid the price for that abuse, didn't I?" she asked bleakly.

Joyce shook her head. "It contributed to the problem, but it certainly wasn't the sole reason. There were a lot of factors leading up to your miscarriage." She scribbled

129

across the patient's progress chart. "I'll expect you in my office next week. Don't be alarmed if you experience some spotting. If there's anything heavier, call me immediately. I also expect you to take some time off and get plenty of rest."

"There won't be any problem there," Ryan announced, entering the room.

"Oh? Are you going to hog-tie me to the bed?" Keri asked pertly.

Ryan grinned. Upon seeing that the color had returned to Keri's face and that she had regained her high-spirited nature, his own spirits were lifted. "That's a little extreme for my taste." He turned to Joyce. "Lacy and I are going away for two weeks, beginning Monday. There's plenty of room, so there isn't any reason why Keri can't come along and enjoy some peace and quiet," he suggested smoothly.

Keri's mouth dropped open in shock. He was doing it again! "Oh, yes there is," she stated defiantly. "The best reason in the world."

"Which is . . . ?" Ryan asked.

"I don't care to go!" Keri announced.

## CHAPTER EIGHT

"He wouldn't listen to me!" Keri wailed to Joyce the next morning. "All he did was stand there with that silly smirk on his face and tell me to be sure to pack casual clothing only."

"That sounds like Ryan," Joyce agreed blandly, crossing her arms in front of her.

Keri closed her eyes and counted to ten, then began counting to ten again.

"I can't take him anymore," she moaned, dropping onto the bed. "Here I was, enjoying my life, proud of my business, happy with myself, and he had to come along and upset everything."

"He certainly hasn't made your life boring, has he?" Joyce guessed.

Keri cast her a baleful look. "I'm taking the Fifth," she muttered.

"Fifth of what?" Ryan walked into the room. "Did you release her, Warden?" he asked Joyce.

"She's signed, sealed, and now delivered."

"I am getting tired of people talking over and around me," Keri said, speaking to no one in particular. She was beginning to dislike Ryan. She disliked the way his worn jeans fit snugly over his hips and thighs and outlined his small, hard buttocks. Not to mention the way his knit shirt fitted his chest and shoulders like a second skin. Keri wished he didn't look so damned sexy!

In the meantime Ryan was looking Keri over just as carefully. She still looked drawn and strained from her ordeal, but to him she could never look lovelier. Her coral-colored linen pants and striped shirt gave much-needed color to her face. For the past few days he had wrestled with his inner self over the thought of some other man making love to Keri. His nights were hours of torture as he paced his bedroom carpet, picturing the two of them in bed, her body naked, flushed with the heat of lust, her lips moist and parted, waiting for his kiss. Even now Ryan could feel his stomach muscles contracting. He had to remind himself that he would have to go slow with Keri or lose her forever.

At first Ryan had thought of just stepping out of Keri's life. After all, she didn't want him around, and he didn't need to be hit over the head to take a hint. That was until the first time he kissed her thoroughly and she had tentatively responded. Ryan was hooked after that. All he wanted was to free Keri from her fears for her to respond to him completely. He had sensed that her mind was wary of him as a man. But he knew her body wanted to accept him.

That was why Ryan was hoping that two weeks away from Tucson would help Keri regain her trust in men.

"All ready to leave?" he inquired politely.

"You tell me," Keri retorted crossly, her eyes snapping blue flames at him.

Ryan grinned. A sassy Keri he could handle.

Ten minutes later Keri had taken care of her hospital bill and a nurse had wheeled her outside, where Ryan's Porsche was waiting.

"Didn't you have a larger car when you brought me here?" Keri asked curiously, once she had been carefully deposited in the passenger seat. She vaguely remembered Ryan cradling her in his arms during the painful drive to the hospital. What also tugged at the far reaches of her memory were snatches of words—her pleas to Ryan and his soft-spoken reassurances that he'd never leave her.

Ryan nodded. "I'm having some touch-up work done on it," he replied, turning on the ignition and putting the car in gear.

The drive to Keri's house was quiet except for the background music from the radio.

Keri stepped inside the living room. She found a neatly stacked pile of mail on top of her coffee table. It wasn't difficult to guess who had placed it there.

"I didn't think you'd mind if I brought your mail in," Ryan said from behind her.

She shook her head in mute disbelief. "Tell me something, Ryan." Keri looked at him with a vague smile. "I suppose I can argue, yell my lungs out, and stamp my feet in a temper tantrum, but I'll still be accompanying you and Lacy on your vacation, right?"

Ryan breathed a silent sigh of relief. It looked as if she wasn't going to put up too much of an argument.

"I'm going to let you rest," Ryan said as he prepared to take his leave.

"Rest!" Keri's eyes almost bugged out. "That's all I've done lately."

"Good, then you've had enough practice to get it right." He headed for the door. "How about dinner tonight?"

She paused. "No pizza," she stated.

"No pizza."

133

"I'll be ready at seven." After all, Keri had to make at least one decision.

"Rest," Ryan said as he walked out the door.

Keri fixed herself a large cold soft drink and carried it upstairs along with her tote bag. Unpacking didn't take long; neither did her call to her office. She was assured that all was going well and not to worry.

Keri undressed and put on a floor-length cotton robe. She suddenly felt very tired and couldn't remember when her bed had looked as inviting as it did now.

Once settled between the cool sheets, she curled up on her side and focused her thoughts on what was rapidly becoming her favorite subject—Ryan.

"Because I love you," he had told her that evening in the hospital.

"No," she uttered in a fierce whisper. "He's been trying to plow through my life from that first day, and for some insane reason I've let him!" Keri fastened her eyes on some invisible spot on the wall and soon dozed off.

Ryan arrived promptly at seven and took Keri to a restaurant known for grilling its steaks over mesquite wood.

The conversation was kept casual and entirely dominated by Ryan, but it didn't matter to Keri. She was finally discovering how enjoyable it could be to have a man pay attention to her.

"You haven't mentioned where I'm to take the balance of my rest cure," Keri chided lightly as they relaxed after dinner with coffee for her and a brandy for Ryan.

"No more arguments about going?" He arched a questioning eyebrow.

Keri's eyes never wavered from Ryan's gaze. This was going to be a big step for her.

"Arguing with you, Ryan Kincaid, is like talking to the wind." Keri smiled. "I'm sure it'll be a snowy day in July when I win an argument with you."

He threw his head back and laughed, drawing more than one interested pair of feminine eyes. Keri doubted that Ryan could walk into any room and not have at least one admirer of the opposite sex.

Keri lay her head against the headrest of her seat during the drive home. She may have taken a nap that afternoon, but that seemed a long time ago. It was barely ten-thirty, and she felt as if she had been out all night. She didn't think Ryan would stay very long when they reached her house. His perception of her physical state had always been accurate.

"I'll be busy tying up loose ends until Monday," Ryan told Keri after she had unlocked her front door. "We'll pick you up at eight that morning."

"Will I need my passport?" she asked lightly.

His fingertips gently kneaded her shoulders. "Casual clothing and a couple of dressy dresses," he told her. His expression darkened. "I'm only patient to a point, Keri. Soon the day will come when we'll have to have our talk."

Keri swallowed the lump in her throat. "Oh, Ryan"— her voice broke—"where were you six months ago?"

His smile relaxed his dark features. "Watching Jason attend business breakfasts. If only I had known then . . ." he murmured, brushing her lips with his own.

A strange heat invaded Keri's body at Ryan's gentle, butterfly kisses. "You're dangerous," she said, then laughed shakily.

"Umm, not really." He proceeded to nibble along her jaw.

"Ryan!" Her plea ended almost as a wail.

He could sense the fear still lurking in her depths and silently cursed himself for being the cause. He released her and stepped back, frowning at the conflicting emotions crossing her face. "Oh, Keri," he whispered huskily, touching the petal-soft skin of her cheek with trembling fingers. "Haven't you realized yet that I'd never do anything to hurt you?"

She nodded once. "I'm agreeing to go with you and Lacy, aren't I?" she replied with quivering lips, still moist from his kiss.

"I'll call you in the next day or so," he promised after he had kissed her lips all too briefly.

Keri went up to bed, still wondering if she might have taken leave of her senses. That was the only explanation for her behavior lately! She knew she needed to discuss her feelings about Ryan with someone and could think of only one person.

"I'm glad to see that you're looking better," Cassie greeted Keri two days later, Keri having invited her to lunch.

"I'm feeling better too. How are you doing?" Keri went into the kitchen to pour two glasses of white wine.

"Fine. My assignment with Ryan was supposed to end last Friday, but he asked if I'd stay until after he got back from his vacation." Cassie seated herself at the round table.

"Does he still want you to stay permanently?"

Cassie nodded, accepting the chilled glass. "But I think he'll be happy with Martha." Martha was the secretary Ryan had hired recently.

"Oh? What's she like?" Keri asked casually, picking up the pot holders from the counter. She concentrated on opening the oven door and withdrawing a pan of mushroom quiche.

Cassie grinned. "She's in her early fifties and has the personality of a Marine drill sergeant."

Keri blushed, seeing the assessing look on Cassie's face.

"He's truly hooked, Keri," Cassie pointed out.

Keri placed the hot pan on a ceramic trivet on the table and cut two pieces. After serving those, she took a tossed salad out of the refrigerator.

"Does this lunch invitation have something to do with Ryan?" Cassie asked, picking up the salad tongs.

Keri nodded. "He . . . ah . . ." She fiddled with her wineglass until Cassie pushed it out of her reach. "He's asked me to go away with him and his daughter," she finally mumbled.

Cassie sat back and exhaled a deep breath. "Now, why am I not surprised?" she mused. "And you're going, of course."

"Has anyone ever said no to Ryan?" Keri asked wryly.

"Me," she quipped. "And I bet you have too. Except on this. How do you feel about going?"

"Confused," Keri confessed.

Cassie took several bites before talking. "I've had a good opportunity to observe Ryan these past few weeks, and one thing I can say honestly is that he's a man to respect and trust. A woman under his protection would be greatly cherished."

*Cherished.* There was a word Keri hadn't thought of before in conjunction with Ryan. Yet, she should have, because that was exactly how he had treated her—as someone to be cherished.

"He puzzles me, Cassie," she admitted candidly, "and infuriates me and makes me crazy."

"And . . . ?" she prompted.

Keri shook her head, unable to describe her feelings for Ryan. "I'm going with him and Lacy because, ironically, Ryan still leaves me in control of the situation—although he does seem to get his way quite easily," she added.

"Damn the torpedoes; full speed ahead," Cassie chanted.

"Yeah, that's Ryan all right," Keri acknowledged dryly, sitting back in her chair and sipping her wine.

Cassie speared a tomato wedge and brought it to her lips. "If I didn't know better, I'd swear that you have more than a passing interest in the illustrious Mr. Kincaid."

"But I shouldn't!" Keri protested without denying Cassie's teasing statement. Her eyes betrayed a vulnerability she hadn't allowed to surface for a long time. "Too much has happened, Cassie."

The blond woman considered her friend thoughtfully. She knew that Keri was still keeping a lot of hurt inside, and Cassie could only hope that Ryan would be the one to heal the wounds.

Keri inspected her nails and idly noticed that the polish was chipped on several of them.

"Of course, I shouldn't worry with his daughter along as chaperone," she said distractedly.

"When you put it that way, it doesn't sound as much fun."

Keri giggled at Cassie's dry quip. She blamed her uncharacteristic giggle on the glass and a half of wine she had consumed during lunch.

"I think that my life is taking another turn." She finished the last bite of her quiche.

"Welcome to the club." Cassie's fingers toyed with the stem of her wineglass. "Barb mentioned that you're going to hire another consultant."

"Uh-huh." Keri got up and went over to the refrigerator to retrieve the sour-cream blueberry pie she had picked up for dessert. "We've gotten quite a few new clients in the past month and we need the extra help."

"Would you consider someone without previous agency experience?" Cassie asked casually.

Keri turned around, still holding the pie server in one hand. "Do you mean *you*'re interested in the job?"

Cassie laughed at the surprised expression on Keri's face. "I know I vowed I'd never work at one position on a permanent basis again, but your work is never the same two days in a row."

"That's true," Keri agreed readily. She didn't take long to decide. "Do you want to start after you finish at Kin-Cal?"

Cassie's eyes widened. "That's all there is to it?"

"Cassie, you've worked for me since I opened the agency. You probably know as much, if not more, about many of the clients," Keri told her. "If you want to join the madhouse in the office, you're certainly hired. I'll just have to give up my best temp," she joked.

The balance of their time together was spent with Keri explaining to Cassie the duties of a personnel consultant after Keri had placed a call to Barb to inform her that the vacant position in their office had been filled.

Ryan's absorption with the view from his office window was purely superficial. His thoughts were centered on a wide-eyed, golden-haired beauty whose one aim in life seemed to be to drive him crazy.

His expression darkened as he remembered an almost hysterical Keri clutching him and begging him not to let her die. He'd remember that day for as long as he lived. He'd never be able to forget the abject horror on Keri's face when she discovered the blood on her pants, or the pain-filled cries she uttered in fear of death overtaking her. During that time Ryan would have fought even the gods to keep Keri with him.

"I believe the old-fashioned way of putting it is that I'm besotted with her," he muttered to himself, gazing sourly at the stack of paperwork on his desk. It didn't help to remind himself that everything had to be gone over before he left on Monday, meaning that there was a weekend of hard work ahead of him.

There were two things about Keri that Ryan would always remember: her beautiful eyes and her equally beautiful mouth. Oh, how that mouth felt under his—the moist lips that tasted like some kind of sensuous fruit. But he knew it was her eyes with their incredible color that had captivated him first.

Ryan was glad that Keri had agreed to accompany Lacy and him on their trip. He had no ulterior motives. Oh, sure, he wanted to make love to her—he'd be a fool to claim otherwise—but he knew he would have to give her time, not only because of her emotional well-being, but for health reasons also.

He smiled at the thought of two weeks spent with his two favorite women. They were fourteen days he was greatly looking forward to.

Keri knew there was one more person she would have

to tell about her impromptu vacation. What surprised her the most was Amanda's reaction.

"I'm glad to see that you've found a man who can handle you," the older woman said bluntly during their telephone conversation on Saturday evening. "You go and enjoy yourself."

Keri couldn't help but tease her sister. "I thought you didn't approve of an unmarried couple going off together."

"No man takes his fifteen-year-old daughter along if he's planning X-rated activities," Amanda retorted. "Besides, if you had your way, you'd be back in your office first thing Monday, insisting on taking on ten jobs at once. I doubt Ryan will allow you to do more than pick up your fork during your meals."

"Well, it's nice to know that I have everyone's blessing," Keri said, laughing softly.

## CHAPTER NINE

Late on Monday morning Keri stood on a balcony overlooking a white sandy beach and the Pacific Ocean.

She had been quite surprised when Ryan picked her up that morning and then the three drove to the airport. "Company jet?" Keri asked when Ryan ushered her and Lacy into the small Lear jet.

He nodded. "Jason's idea, actually, after we started acquiring properties outside the state."

"And our destination?"

"San Diego!" Lacy declared excitedly, bouncing onto one of the seats, which resembled easy chairs, and tossing her hair away from her face.

Keri turned to Ryan, who shrugged. "I may have to make a few business calls while we're there," he explained, placing his briefcase on a round table near the front of the cabin.

"Where are we staying?" she asked curiously.

"In a time-share condominium Jason is part owner of," Ryan explained.

"As long as there's plenty of guys around," Lacy mused, buckling her seat belt.

Ryan sighed. This was his first year as a frazzled father dealing with a boy-crazy daughter.

The flight passed uneventfully with Lacy reading her

favorite teen gossip magazine and Keri playing gin rummy with Ryan. At the airport he loaded them into the rental car he had arranged for and headed for the beach area and the elegant condominium building.

The split-level condo was tastefully decorated in cream and rust with touches of navy for accent. The bedroom Keri and Lacy were to share boasted two king-size beds and a large adjoining bathroom. French doors opened out onto a wide balcony, where Keri was now standing.

Ryan stepped out onto the balcony to stand beside her. "Does it meet with your approval?"

She turned and presented him with a bright smile. "Oh, yes. It's beautiful here."

"How come you get that fantastic bedroom upstairs while we're down here?" Lacy demanded, running into the room.

"Because I'm the oldest, minx."

Lacy grimaced. "He always comes up with the most logical answers," she complained to Keri, then turned back to her father. "Are we going to the beach now?"

"What about some lunch first?" Ryan suggested.

"Then the beach?" Lacy persisted.

"It's a shame there's no sun and sand back home," he said, wrapping a hand around his daughter's nape.

"Not like here," she protested.

"The beach after lunch," he agreed.

Twenty minutes later they were seated in a seafood restaurant on Mission Bay. Keri chose crab salad, Lacy ordered shrimp salad, and Ryan selected fried clams.

Keri was surprised to discover that Lacy didn't mind her presence a bit during what should have been a private time for the young girl and her father. Instead, Lacy was busy enjoying herself by gazing around the restaurant and smiling at any male over the age of sixteen.

"She's just feeling her power," Keri murmured to Ryan, who was looking disgruntled at his daughter's audacious manner.

"Terrific," he muttered into his plate.

After they ate, Lacy reminded her father of his promise to go to the beach. Once they had entered the apartment, Lacy tore into the bedroom to change into her bathing suit.

"I don't suppose you'd be willing to stay behind for a nap while she goes down to the beach?" Ryan asked wistfully.

Keri shook her head. "The beach sounds like an excellent idea." She moved to follow Lacy.

"Hmm, I thought you'd say that," he grumbled good-naturedly, heading for the spiral staircase that led to his bedroom.

Lacy had already changed into a French-cut bikini and twisted her hair on top of her head by the time Keri entered the bedroom.

"Did you see all those gorgeous hunks out there?" Lacy chattered, dumping a bottle of suntan oil and other necessities into a canvas tote bag.

"I'm afraid they were a little young for me," Keri replied, picking up her bathing suit and walking into the bathroom. In no time she was in her black-and-peacock-blue one-piece suit with her hair pulled back in a braid.

*"What in the hell is that?"* Ryan demanded when Lacy walked into the living room with Keri following.

Lacy looked down at herself. "My suit?"

*"Suit?"* he thundered. "That's not a suit. There's only a couple of pieces of string to it!"

"Oh, Daddy," she protested in a long-suffering tone. "This suit is positively old-fashioned compared to some of my friends'."

Ryan took deep breaths to control his temper. "You're not leaving here until you change into something that covers you more. Say, from neck to knees."

*"Daddy!"* Lacy wailed.

"Ryan," Keri interjected quietly, "it's not as if she's revealing anything obvious. And she's right: I've seen plenty of teenagers in less than what she's wearing."

He thrust his fingers through his hair in an agitated gesture. "I've seen strippers wear more," he muttered, then glared at his daughter. "At least wear something over it until we reach the beach. I'd hate to have to bail you out because you've been arrested for indecent exposure," he grumbled, jerking a navy T-shirt over his head.

Keri turned her head to hide her smile. What would Ryan say when she pulled off her terry-cloth shirt?

Ryan was silent during the elevator ride down to the lobby.

"Uh, I can't die of thirst out there, can I?" Lacy's eyes sparkled as she held out her hand to her father.

"One thing after another," Ryan muttered amiably, handing Lacy a fistful of change. "Why don't you get something for Keri and me too? We'll go and stake out a stretch of sand."

As they walked outside in the glaring sunshine Ryan slipped on his sunglasses and held out a hand for Keri's string tote bag. He put his hand on the back of her neck and squeezed lightly. "I'm glad you came, Keri," he said quietly.

She continued to look straight ahead. "So am I." Her murmur barely reached his ears.

Ryan reached an unoccupied area close to the water yet far enough back for comfort, and dropped his towel and Keri's bag. He pulled off his T-shirt and placed it, too, on the hot sand.

Keri kept sneaking peeks at Ryan's well-toned body, which was now garbed only in navy swim briefs.

"See anything you like?"

She blushed at his amused tone. Affecting an air of indifference, she looked around the beach at the male half of the population, a majority of which appeared to be under the age of twenty-one.

"Hmm, there are a few, as long as I don't mind someone who probably only shaves once a week," Keri declared airily.

"Okay, you've made your point." Ryan sounded disgruntled as he snapped the beach towels in the air before laying them out on the sand. He flopped down on his towel and looked up at her expectantly. "Does that top come off?"

"Sure does." Keri grabbed the hem of her shirt and slowly pulled it up and over her head.

Ryan felt as if he had been poleaxed. Keri's suit may have been a one-piece, but the legs were French-cut, the back almost nonexistent except for string ties, and a strip of material covering her buttocks.

"At least the front is pretty well covered," he mumbled, focusing on the full swells of her breasts.

"Are you going to make me go upstairs and change?" Keri teased, dropping to her knees on her towel.

Ryan's eyes darkened, but not with anger. "If I hustled you upstairs, it wouldn't be to change your clothes."

"Ryan . . ." she managed to say, her lips suddenly

146

dry. Their eyes bored into each other's as if to guess the secrets of the mind . . . and the soul.

Lacy's exuberant voice intruded. "Okay, break it up."

"Don't drop the soda," Ryan ordered lazily, taking two of the icy cans from his daughter.

"Isn't this wonderful?" Lacy mused happily, turning around in a circle.

Ryan sighed audibly. "Sit down before you make us dizzy."

Lacy sat cross-legged on her towel and pulled the aluminum tab on her can of diet soda. "I'm not a little girl anymore, Dad," she informed him. "I even know about sex."

Ryan choked on his drink. "As long as it's theory only," he insisted in a stern voice, spearing his daughter with a fierce look.

"Well, Mom said she'd take me to the doctor for the pill if I wanted it."

Ryan choked again. "I'm going to have a talk with Stella when we get back," he muttered darkly. His displeasure was further heightened when a young man hesitantly approached Lacy. "What do you want?"

"*Daddy!*" Lacy whispered in warning, then flashed a bright smile at the lanky teenager. "Hi."

"We—ah—" He shot a wary glance at the still-scowling Ryan. "We need another person to play on our side in volleyball and I—ah—I wondered if you'd like to play." He nodded toward a group of kids gathered around a nearby volleyball net.

"Sure," Lacy accepted happily, jumping to her feet.

"Leave the shirt on," Ryan advised sardonically when Lacy prepared to peel off her shirt. "I'd hate for you to

147

get a sunburn your first day out," he told her, ignoring her dark tan.

"Ryan"—Keri's eyes danced with amusement at this glimpse of the highly protective father—"Lacy won't be more than fifty yards away."

"Yes, ma'am." The boy clearly guessed he had an ally. "We just thought your daughter might like to play."

Keri watched them lope across the sand. "Daughter," she repeated numbly. "Daughter. I'm not old enough to have a fifteen-year-old daughter."

"Sure you are." Ryan's lips twitched. It was nice to see the tables turned on someone else.

"No I'm not!" Keri argued, glaring daggers at Ryan. Her eyes swung past and settled on a young couple erecting a beach umbrella in the sand and setting up a portable baby's playpen. Her face whitened and her hand fluttered over her stomach momentarily. "I—" She began to rise, prepared to escape from the domestic sight before her.

But Ryan had seen it too. In one lightning-fast move he had taken hold of Keri's hand and refused to allow her to get up.

"No, Keri." He spoke gently but firmly. "Your baby's gone and nothing can change that. But you're here and you're going to keep on surviving."

Her eyes shimmered. "Let me go, Ryan," she pleaded softly, pulling away without success.

He shook his head. "First we're going to go in the water so that I can cool off after seeing you in that suit." He stood up and pulled Keri to her feet. A gentle tug of his hand had her walking across the sand with him.

For the balance of the afternoon Ryan made sure that Keri had no time to feel sorry for herself. He taught her to bodysurf and initiated a water fight—anything to keep her mind occupied. He had another reason for his actions: He wanted to see her laugh.

"Hey, no fair!" Keri shouted when Ryan ducked under the water again.

"Sure it is," he retorted.

Later, when they walked back to their towels, Ryan's arm encircled Keri's waist.

"Whew!" Ryan flopped onto his towel and searched for his can of soda.

"That's mine," Keri told him, picking up her towel and drying her arms and shoulders.

He flashed her a wicked grin and took another sip. "I know."

An hour later Ryan had to drag Lacy away from her newfound friends so that they could go upstairs to dress for dinner and a concert Ryan had procured tickets for.

"Concert!" Lacy scoffed, heading for the bedroom. "How utterly boring."

"Hurry up with your shower," Ryan ordered lightheartedly. "Since Keri's being nice enough to let you go first, the least you can do is finish up quickly. Or," he said to Keri, his voice lowered, even though Lacy had closed the bedroom door after her, "you can share my shower. I'm a generous guy." He nuzzled her ear, working his way down to the lobe. He nipped it gently. "I'll wash your back and you can wash mine."

Keri closed her eyes. The heat rising in her body wasn't due to the warm temperature. "Please don't do this, Ryan," she whispered.

His hands found her waist and turned her to face him. "No one has ever said my name the way you do." Those same hands now rested lightly on her hips. "Say it

149

again," he instructed huskily, bringing his mouth to a fraction of an inch away from hers.

"Ryan," Keri whispered, watching his mouth slowly lower until their lips barely touched. Their breaths mingled. "Ryan . . . Ry—" She was cut off by the abrupt movement of his mouth covering hers.

The hardened tip of Ryan's tongue plunged into the moist interior of Keri's mouth. Each thrust and withdrawal was calculated to mimic the lovemaking he would have preferred to be performing on the king-size bed upstairs. He cupped the rounded skin of her buttocks and pulled her closer to him, wanting her to feel the full impact of his arousal.

"Hold me, Keri," he murmured against her lips, which were shining from his kiss. "Touch me," he pleaded against the velvety soft skin of her neck. "Feel me against you." He thrust his hips suggestively against hers. "Oh, Keri, love, we could be so good together," he groaned.

Keri gasped when Ryan's hand covered her right breast, the thumb caressing her hardened nipple. The shock sent heat waves through the center of her body. She stroked the slightly rough skin of his nape with her fingertips, then moved down to his shoulders, finding downy hairs covering the taut skin. The coarse hair on his chest teased the sensitive skin above the neckline of her suit.

"Damn," Ryan swore softly, burying his face against Keri's throat, his tongue moving languidly.

"Wha—?" She was still in a fog.

"The shower just stopped"—he stepped back but kept a light hold of her forearms until her head stopped whirling—"and Lacy will be wondering what has happened to you." Ryan's jaw clenched in frustration. "If I had an ounce of sense, I'd lock her in that room and carry you up to my bed."

Keri shook her head, trying to clear her hazy brain. "Please, Ryan, don't push me."

"Will you ever trust me?" he demanded hoarsely. Even now he could sense her withdrawing from him.

She looked away and pulled free from his grasp. The bedroom door closed softly after her.

"Damn!" Ryan pounded his fist into his palm. *One way or another, I'm going to find out what frightens her.*

Lacy could sense a new tension between the two adults that evening and wisely kept silent when necessary. Her sense of humor, inherited from her father, surfaced only once. At the concert Lacy took an aisle seat so that Keri and Ryan sat next to each other.

The tension remained during the next few days. Ryan was polite and correct to Keri during their trip to the zoo. Even the wild-animal park was viewed in a state of siege. And each evening, his whispered words to Keri were the same: "You can't hold out forever, Keri. I intend to find out sooner or later."

They spent another afternoon lazing on the beach, with Lacy studying fashion magazines. "This one has that article on businesswomen I told you about." She handed one of the magazines to Keri.

"Oh?" Keri perused some of the articles listed on the cover. Then suddenly her face paled. "Excuse me," she muttered and jumped up, running back to the building.

"Where's Keri going?" Ryan asked as he returned from a swim.

"I don't know." Lacy shrugged. "I guess she wasn't interested in an article I was showing her."

Ryan picked up the magazine. The lead articles dealt with battered wives; women running their own businesses; women dealing with the deaths of their mates; "social" rape; and women in politics.

"Isn't this a little too adult for you?" Ryan asked Lacy.

She arched her eyebrows. "Oh, Daddy, I know much more than you give me credit for."

"That's what I'm afraid of," he muttered, dropping the magazine. He looked up toward the building. He let Keri run this time.

Keri stood under a steaming hot shower. She was hoping that if she stood there long enough, her tense muscles would loosen.

*Tell him!* her mind screamed. *He'll keep the nightmares away. Let Ryan heal my pain.* But all she did was remain under the hot water.

That evening Ryan excused himself after dinner, saying he was meeting someone regarding business.

Keri and Lacy watched a movie on TV and gave each other a manicure and pedicure.

Lacy dropped her bomb with casual aplomb: "Why aren't you and Dad sleeping together?"

"Are you sure you're only fifteen?" Keri asked once she'd regained her voice.

"Mom's boyfriends are always sleeping over." The young girl selected a bright rose-colored nail polish.

"Your father and I don't have that kind of relationship," Keri finally murmured, deciding that her face was as red as the bottle of polish she held.

"Well, then, I just want you to know that you have my blessing," Lacy declared.

Keri held up her glass of soda in a toast. "Thank you,

Mother," she intoned, smiling, but Lacy's words stayed with her for the rest of the evening.

Ryan was late returning that evening. Keri lay awake in her bed and heard the soft opening and closing of the front door. A clinking of glass was heard: He must have poured himself a drink. Then another. Did that mean his business meeting hadn't gone well, or was there another reason? After a while, she could hear the muted click of the light switch and footsteps climbing the stairs to a lonely bed.

Keri curled up on her side to look out the open French doors. She could just barely make out the sounds of running water and drawers opening and closing. Then silence.

She thought about a lot of things as she lay there. The first time she had seen Ryan, the first time he had kissed her, and the many times he had been there when she needed someone. She especially remembered his gentleness and strength during her miscarriage, not to mention the time he had told her he loved her. Her eyes burned with unshed tears.

She had a decision to make. She turned over and studied a sleeping Lacy, who lay sprawled on her stomach.

Keri carefully pushed the covers down and sat up. She held her breath when Lacy shifted slightly. She waited another moment before moving again. Silently she crept out of the room and made sure the door was securely closed after her.

Keri paused a moment before gliding across the darkened living room to the stairs. When she reached the top of the stairs, she was facing his bed.

"Lacy?" Ryan sat up, the sheets a pale blur against his

bare skin. He leaned forward in order to see his visitor better. "Keri, is something wrong?"

She shook her head, unable to say anything.

"Keri." His voice softened. "Are you all right? I may be a lot of things, but I can't see in the dark. You're going to have to say something."

Keri walked forward until she reached the bed. Whether the tremors shooting through her body were due to the cool night air or fear, she didn't know.

"Ryan"—she held out her hand—"please make love to me."

His brow knit in confusion. "Keri, I . . ." He shook his head. He reached up to take her hand and pull her down beside him.

"Isn't this what you've wanted all along?" she cried. "Well, I'm here." She slipped her arms around him and kissed him fervently.

At first Ryan crushed Keri against him in passionate response. Then, just as suddenly, he held her away from him.

"What's wrong?" Keri asked, twisting in his arms.

"This isn't the place, Keri," he objected gently. "Not when my daughter is sleeping downstairs. Not this way, love."

She shook her head rapidly. "But, Ryan . . ."

He pulled her against him, wrapping his arms around her and arranging the covers over them both.

"Oh, Keri," he sighed. "You're still confused, aren't you?"

She luxuriated in the warmth of his embrace. "I think I love you, Ryan," she whispered, admitting what had been deep in her heart for a long time.

"Ahhh." Ryan let out a whoosh of air. "You sure pick a hell of a time to tell me."

She shifted her weight and stretched her legs out alongside his.

"Are you also ready to trust me, Keri?" he inquired quietly.

Keri stiffened; the silence in the room was deafening. Then she began a painful story: "Larry, the man who was at my house that day was the father. He . . . ah . . . I hadn't told him about the baby."

"Where did you meet him?"

"Ironically, at the businessman's breakfast a little over four months ago," she said.

Ryan grunted.

Keri took a deep breath. "We began dating and I found him to be a nice man, although his behavior was erratic at times."

"What happened?" Ryan wasn't sure he wanted to hear this.

Keri hesitated, choosing her words carefully. "It was the fourth time we had gone out, and I invited Larry in for coffee." She shuddered, not wanting to continue but knowing she had to. She needed to purge the emotional pain. "He started kissing me, but soon he wanted more. He . . . he pulled up my dress and started tearing at my underclothes. I—" She stopped, unable to control her voice. "I kept saying no, but he ignored me. Af-afterwards he left, saying it was a great evening."

Ryan could feel poisonous rage filling his body. The thought of a man forcing any woman against her will angered him. That the woman who had been forced was his Keri was enough to send him into a murderous frenzy. "Why didn't you press charges against him?" he asked. "For God's sake, Keri, the bastard raped you!"

Keri turned and pressed her cheek against his chest. She felt protected with his arms around her. "It's impossible to charge a man with rape when you've seen him socially and you've invited him into your home. In fact, the term is 'social' rape or 'date' rape."

"But it's still rape," Ryan argued forcefully, trying to ignore Keri's arm lying so trustfully across his chest. "People like him should pay."

"Rape is considered to be the use of force," Keri pointed out softly. "He didn't hold a gun to my head; he merely ignored my wishes. I didn't see him after that until he showed up the day of my miscarriage."

"Now I wish that I had broken his face." Ryan's body was tense with anger, and part of that anger was directed at himself. "No wonder you were so scared of me that first night. You were afraid I'd do the same thing."

She nodded.

"Don't take this the wrong way, Keri, but weren't you on the pill?"

"On the advice of my gynecologist, I had gone off it for a few months and had been fitted for a diaphragm," she explained. "I know you can't understand why I didn't have an abortion when I found out I was pregnant, but I just couldn't consider it."

"I should have killed him when I had the chance," Ryan muttered, thinking of many ways to tear a man apart, all illegal.

"No!" She sat up and placed her fingertips over his lips. "I'm just glad that you were there to pick up the pieces."

He framed her face with trembling hands. She meant

so very much to him. "No one will ever hurt you again, Keri," he vowed. *"No one."*

Now so much of it fell into place: Keri's fear of Ryan's passionate side and of his touching her intimately; her reaction toward Larry that day and why she had left the beach so abruptly. The article on social rape had brought it all back to her.

"And now you are never to think or worry about it again." Ryan's tongue had found the corner of Keri's mouth. "I'll make sure to keep your mind concentrated strictly on other people. One in particular."

Keri sat up and half turned to look at him in the dim light. "You still want to see me?"

"Of course I do. What made you think I wouldn't?"

"Well, because of what happened," Keri mumbled.

Ryan's fingers glided through her hair. "A situation occurred in which you weren't allowed to control your life. That shouldn't happen to anyone. Some men can only think with certain parts of their anatomy. Hopefully the day will come when they get punished."

"Hopefully they'll boil him in oil," Keri spat out.

"My bloodthirsty darling." Ryan chuckled, drawing her closer, which he soon realized was a mistake. Now wasn't the time to think of how her skin smelled warm and womanly, of how her hair felt like the rarest silk against his cheek, of how her breath was moist on his chest, of how her nightgown could hide her slender body but couldn't disguise the curves and valleys his hands itched to explore. "Stop that," he ordered thickly.

Keri stopped idly combing the hair on Ryan's chest with her fingers. She didn't want to stop touching him. She was happy that her fear had disappeared when she told him the whole story about Larry. She had a pretty

157

good idea that Ryan would do anything in his power to ensure that her pain never returned.

"Keri, you're going to have to leave." There was a curious choking sound in Ryan's voice. He pushed her upright. "Damnit, if you don't leave now, I won't be able to let you go."

She smiled at his admission of how little self-control he had where she was concerned. While testing that control was a heady thought, Keri knew that her willpower wasn't all that strong either. And Ryan was correct: Lacy had to be considered.

"You're a very special man, Ryan Kincaid." She touched his face with inquiring fingers.

He brought her fingertips to his lips and nibbled each one. "I'm pleased to hear that you've finally realized that," he murmured.

"Oh, I think I've been telling myself that all along. All I had to do was believe it." Keri climbed off the bed, but Ryan pulled her down for one heart-stopping kiss, his tongue plunging deeply. When he finally released her, her knees were shaky and his breathing was rough and labored.

"Now get out of here," he demanded affectionately. "As it is, I'm probably going to have to take a long, cold shower before I get any sleep."

Keri's heart felt so much lighter. "Let me know if you need your back scrubbed," she teased from the top of the stairs.

When she returned to her bed, she fell to sleep instantly, while Ryan lay awake cursing his strong principles that had just sent her back to bed.

## CHAPTER TEN

Lacy was astute enough to see the change between Keri and Ryan during their last week in San Diego. There were the intimate little smiles they shared, the ways they always seemed to find reasons to touch each other, the murmured conversations.

"Lacy asked me why we weren't sleeping together," Keri told Ryan one afternoon while they lay on the beach and the young girl had been commandeered for a volleyball game.

Ryan groaned. "I'm surprised every hair on my head isn't gray."

"No, there's just a very sexy smattering," she teased, running her fingers through the object of their conversation. "Lacy also gave us her blessing," she added.

"I don't think I'll survive these next ten years. What happened to the pigtails and braces, playing with dolls and playing hopscotch?" Ryan moaned.

"They're pressed in your memory book. Most girls that age experiment," Keri explained.

Ryan's eyes spelled danger for any of the young boys near his daughter. "Just as long as she doesn't experiment with any of those adolescent sex maniacs."

"Not that kind of experiment, dolt," Keri chided, tugging on his earlobe. "She's beginning to feel her power as a member of the feminine sex. And you should feel happy that she doesn't resent me being here. Most girls her age wouldn't appreciate sharing their fathers and would take every opportunity to make everyone's life miserable."

"Well, then, I guess I'd better keep her." Ryan captured Keri's marauding hand and laced her fingers through his. "And you, too," he added sincerely, meeting her laughing eyes with his serious ones.

Keri smiled and pressed a light kiss on Ryan's mouth. "I always wondered what it would be like to be adopted," she murmured, lingering to savor the salty taste of his lips from his recent dip in the ocean.

"Adoption wasn't quite what I had in mind." His hand surreptitiously crept up to stroke her hip. "And if you continue with these sexy little pranks of yours, you're going to find yourself slung over my shoulder and carried up to the apartment for an afternoon of decadent pleasure."

A searing thrill shot through her at the image of that. "What about Lacy?" She changed her position slightly so that Ryan's hand now glided over her thigh and crept closer along her sensitive skin. Luckily, given the position they were lying in, no one could see exactly where their hands were.

"Let her find her own guy," Ryan murmured, sucking in his breath when Keri's fingertip toyed with his navel. "Of course, she'll have to wait until she's twenty-five or so."

"Did you?" She closed her eyes in sensual enjoyment of Ryan's exploring fingertips tracing the elastic edge of her swimsuit.

"Did I what?" He breathed in sharply when her hand

passed lightly over the front of his swim briefs, which suddenly felt too snug for comfort.

"Wait until you were twenty-five?" Keri inched closer to Ryan until their thighs brushed against each other.

"Are you kidding?" Ryan replied hoarsely, wanting nothing more than to ease the ache Keri had generated with her teasing hands.

"Are you two going to lie there and do nothing all day or are you coming swimming?" Lacy demanded from above.

"Lie here and do nothing," he muttered, adding to Keri under his breath, "You'd better go on ahead with her. It's going to take me a few minutes to switch from X-rated to G. I'm just glad there's only two days left. I don't think I can survive much longer."

Privately, Keri didn't think she could either.

If Ryan could have gotten the jet to go any faster, he would have gotten out and pushed. When they reached Tucson, he dropped Lacy off at their house, then drove Keri home.

Ryan dropped Keri's suitcases in the middle of the living room and reached for her. "If I didn't have Lacy at the house tonight, I'd probably settle in for the night."

"Now I know you're crazy," Keri gurgled, lifting her face for his kiss.

"About you I am."

Now all that mattered was the melding of their mouths and the taste of each other.

"I have to go while I still can," Ryan said in a ragged voice, pulling away reluctantly.

"Will I see you soon?" She almost hated herself for asking.

"I'm meeting Jason tomorrow, but I'll try to get away early and stop by here," he promised. "Either way, how about lunch on Monday?"

"Sounds fine."

Except the next day didn't end up as anticipated. Ryan wasn't able to call Keri with his apology until late that evening. Lunch was still planned for Monday.

But that didn't come off either.

"I'm sorry, love," Ryan sighed over the phone Monday morning. "As it is, I have just enough time to make my flight to Houston. I'm hoping to be home by the weekend, and you'd better be prepared for a lot of loving."

"Ah, Ryan . . ." She hesitated, unsure of how to tell him.

"Why do I get the idea that your news isn't very good?" he asked with trepidation.

Keri bit her lower lip in indecision. She quickly got up from her chair and closed her office door. "It's something I should have remembered before." She lowered her voice even more, afraid of being overheard.

"Keri, what's wrong?" Ryan asked gently.

"Joyce said that I would have to wait six weeks before I—before we—That is . . ." she stammered.

"I get the message," he hastily reassured her. "And I think it's a good thing I'm going to Houston for a week. I've got to run. I'll call you tonight."

"Is that maidenly blush thanks to someone we both know?" Cassie asked, popping into the office.

"Ryan has to fly to Houston," Keri mused sadly after she made sure her office door was closed. No one but Cassie knew that Keri hadn't gone on her vacation alone.

"How about lunch today, since lover-boy will be out of town?" Cassie suggested.

Keri didn't expect the week to drag into two. Ryan called her every night, and by all rights the telephone lines between Tucson and Houston should have burned to a cinder. As it was, they fairly sizzled!

"Are you in bed?" Ryan asked one night.

"Uh-huh." Keri snuggled under the covers.

"Are you wearing a nightgown or pajamas?"

"Nightgown." She couldn't resist going on. "It's really pretty. Sort of a peach color with lace inserts and a slit to the thigh."

Ryan groaned. "Okay, I get the picture. Let's discuss something else, such as whose house we'll spend the weekend at?" He turned serious. "I want you to do something for me, love. See Joyce this week and make sure you're all right. I'm not asking this for selfish reasons either."

"I had a checkup yesterday," she replied.

"And . . . ?"

"And I'm a very healthy lady," Keri assured him.

"And I'm in another state," Ryan grumbled. "My flight will be coming in next Friday afternoon. I'll pick you up for dinner at seven. Oh, and be sure to take your vitamins," he advised her.

She laughed. "You're impossible."

"That's what they're saying down here too." His voice deepened. "I love you, my stubborn lady."

"And you're very special to me," she said softly. "Good night, Ryan."

With each passing day Keri mulled over her feelings toward Ryan. There was no doubt that he wanted to make love to her and that she felt the same, but what about when the time for intimacy actually came? Would memories of what had happened with Larry intrude when the moment should be just theirs? Ryan was a man with great patience, but how much more would he be able to take? He had revealed to Keri a sensual side of herself that she hadn't known existed. She only hoped that side would surface when the time was right.

By Friday afternoon Keri was figuratively tearing her hair out. Not wanting her office staff to notice her nervousness, she slipped out not long after lunch with the murmured excuse that she had a haircutter's appointment. That wasn't all Keri did to herself. She had also made appointments for a facial and manicure. Not content with just that, she went shopping for a new dress.

Ryan parked the Porsche in front of Keri's house just before seven that evening.

He couldn't remember ever feeling so anxious about taking a woman out. Not even his first date had left him with sweaty palms!

Promptly at seven he rang the doorbell. He could hear footsteps on the tile entryway; then the door opened.

"Hi." Keri smiled a little shyly.

Ryan swallowed. Keri's hair was pinned on top of her head in loose curls that left a few soft tendrils caressing her nape and cheeks. Her lavender-and-white-striped strapless dress was like an ice-cream confection, and her perfume reminded him of a garden in springtime.

"Earth to Ryan." Keri snapped her fingers in front of him to get his attention. "Come in, Ryan."

"I had forgotten how beautiful you are." He drew her

164

to him for a brief but thorough kiss. "We ought to go if we're going to eat."

Inside the Porsche, Ryan cast a rueful eye at the bucket seats. "I should have brought the Audi," he muttered, releasing Keri's hand long enough to shift gears.

"What does a swinging bachelor need with two cars?" she teased.

"The Audi is for impressing new clients and when Lacy has some of her friends with her," he explained.

The restaurant Ryan chose served continental cuisine, and each table was given privacy with strategically placed plants. He wondered if he had made a mistake when various people, male and female alike, stopped by their table to say hello.

"How fast can you eat?" Ryan muttered to Keri after one curvy brunette greeted him with a feline smile and a breathless "Hello, Ryan."

Keri had looked at the woman's figure with something akin to awe. "I don't suppose any of that was padding," she said wistfully.

Ryan frowned at her. "How the hell would I know?"

Keri's smile was pure innocence. "Well, wouldn't you?" She affected the brunette's breathless voice. "Why, Ryan, you're blushing!" She burst out laughing as she noticed the dark red creeping up his neck. She should feel jealousy toward any woman who had shared Ryan's bed, but she was the one sitting beside him now, and she doubted that another woman had heard his declaration of love.

She remembered little of what she ate for dinner. A calorie-laden chocolate mousse was shared between them.

"Some claim that chocolate is an aphrodisiac," he informed her, feeding her a spoonful of the rich dessert.

Keri circled Ryan's wrist with her fingers. "I don't need it," she murmured, taking her time to empty the spoon of its contents.

Ryan never paid a dinner check so fast in his life, although outwardly he remained calm and collected. Once they were seated in the car, he turned to her.

"I thought I'd leave the rest of the evening up to you," he said quietly, silently willing her to meet his eyes. "We could either go dancing or we could go to my place for a brandy."

Keri met Ryan's gaze head on. "I think a brandy sounds just fine," she agreed with a beguiling smile.

They sat in companionable silence during the drive back to Ryan's condo. He parked the car in the garage and led Keri into the house.

When they entered the living room, Ryan gestured toward the couch. "Have a seat," he said. He headed for the bar set up in a corner of the living room.

Keri slipped off her lavender-colored leather heels and curled her legs up under her. She looked up with an earth-shattering smile when Ryan brought over two brandy glasses and held one out to her. "Thank you," she said as she accepted the glass and watched him sit next to her.

Ryan half turned. "Hey, have I told you how much I missed you?" he inquired, toying with a curl.

"Only a thousand times in the past hour," Keri teased. "But tell me more; I love it."

"Your eyes remind me of two very beautiful aquamarines." He leaned over to kiss each closed eyelid. "Your hair always makes me think of a rare antique gold coin and smells like spring." A loose strand found its way to his lips. "And your skin feels like silk." He ran his fingertips over her bare shoulder.

"Yes?" she murmured huskily. "You're not finished, are you?"

"Oh, no." Ryan chuckled. "Let's see, you have a very pert nose—"

"Pert? That makes me sound like a pixie," she protested.

"A *sexy* pixie," he corrected. "Now, be quiet and let me get on with my seducing."

Keri set her glass down on the coffee table and turned back to Ryan, looping her arms around his neck. "Well, then, get on with the seduction," she purred.

"Shut up," Ryan ordered affectionately, pulling her onto his lap. "And kiss me."

Keri had to meet Ryan only halfway. Her mouth was easily parted by his probing tongue.

"Your sweet mouth," he muttered thickly. "Your sweet, sweet mouth."

Keri's fingers dug lightly into Ryan's scalp. A sharp stab of arousal ran through her body during his feverish kisses. Time had whetted their sexual appetites and left them wanting as much of each other as possible.

Her tongue rubbed against his and played its mating game. She swallowed the groan rumbling up from his chest. Keri shivered with anticipation, but Ryan mistook it for fear. He kept his hands on her shoulders and pulled away slightly.

"I don't ever want you to be afraid of me, Keri," he said quietly. "If you become frightened, I want you to tell me. If you want me to stop, I want you to tell me that too. I love you and I won't have my lovemaking bring back your fears."

"I trust you, Ryan," Keri admitted. "I trusted you that night in San Diego. You helped me realize that by talking about what happened with Larry, I was able to put those fears to rest instead of keeping them alive."

Ryan fanned his fingers over Keri's neck and checked her rapidly beating pulse. His palm then moved down over her breast.

"Don't stop, Ryan," she pleaded in a whisper.

He brought her back to him for a soul-devouring kiss. Keri arched up against Ryan's caressing hand.

"Where's the zipper on this thing?" he demanded against her lips.

She sighed with anticipation. "There's no zipper. The top is elasticized."

It didn't take Ryan long to pull the top of Keri's dress down to her waist.

"Beautiful," he said huskily, dipping his head to skate his lips over the rounded globe. "So soft . . . so silky . . ."

A piercing sweetness invaded Keri's body when Ryan's teeth tugged on the nipple. "Make love to me, Ryan," she begged. "Please."

Ryan needed no further invitation. He stood up, keeping Keri in his arms. "Then we may as well continue this upstairs."

Keri snuggled closer and closed her eyes. The trip upstairs to Ryan's bedroom was made in scant seconds. He pulled the covers back on his bed before depositing his bundle.

"You're wearing too many clothes," she said, loosening the navy tie and pulling it from the collar of Ryan's cream silk shirt. Then each button was unfastened with deliberate slowness and she kissed each new area of bare skin. The musky scent of him filled her nostrils, and the tip of her tongue circled one flat nipple, which tautened in response.

*"Keri!"* Ryan groaned. He pushed her away long enough to finish pulling her dress off, leaving her with nothing more than a lacy pair of bikini panties. He quickly shed the rest of his clothes and rejoined her on the bed.

"I didn't think of you as someone who threw his clothes around," Keri commented, curling up against Ryan. She traced every inch of his chest and below with loving fingers.

He gripped her hands to stop her tactile exploration. "I only have so much control, darling," he said. "I want to make this meaningful for you, but I'm going to need some cooperation on your part."

"I thought that was what I was doing." She smiled.

*"Your* idea of cooperation and *mine* don't necessarily agree." Ryan's lips traced an erotic path over her collarbone and along the upper slope of her breast. "I used to lie awake thinking about you lying here in my bed. The real thing is much better." His words were muffled against her skin. His hand caressed the smooth planes of her abdomen. His fingers lightly probed her femininity and found her warm and moist for him. Her hips rolled against his exploring touch.

"That's it, my love," he encouraged in a heavy voice. "Move with me."

Keri's hands roamed over Ryan's shoulders and down his back to his hips. Her legs curled around his calves to draw him closer to her.

"Not yet," Ryan said against her midriff, even as his lips moved lower.

*"Ryan!"* she gasped when his intimate kiss sent a lightning jolt through her body. Her hips were held steady by his hands as his lips, tongue, and gentle nibbles sent her to the edge of a chasm time and time again. When she was finally pushed over the edge, she felt as if her breath had been wrenched from her body. She lay gasping for air even as Ryan moved up her body. He turned away for a moment and fumbled in his night-table drawer. There was a pause before he took her in his arms again.

"I'll always protect you, Keri," he vowed, rolling over onto his back and positioning her body over his, her legs straddling him. One hand moved over her nape and brought her mouth down to his. He guided her gently to him.

Tears filled Keri's eyes as she realized that Ryan was allowing her to control their lovemaking. But her memory of another night and another man filled her mind.

Ryan noted the stiffening of her body immediately and guessed the cause. "Honey"—he framed her face with his palms—"who am I?" he demanded.

"R-Ryan," she choked.

"Say it again," he ordered.

Keri repeated his name.

He kissed her until she first grew limp, then began to move against him. He gripped her hips yet still allowed her to set the rhythm of their lovemaking. As the pace quickened, Ryan's fingers dug deeper into Keri's skin and he thrust deeper into her warmth.

*"Yes!"* he groaned, chanting Keri's name as he prepared to thrust her over the edge. Even as she whimpered for complete satisfaction, he partially withdrew, only to

thrust again and again until they both felt the hot shower of release.

Keri closed her eyes and allowed Ryan to hold her against him. She couldn't remember ever feeling as relaxed as she did then.

"I was right about reality being much better than dreams," Ryan said. He ran his hand over Keri, who still quivered from after shocks. "I'm not letting you get any farther away from me than this."

"Our respective offices might complain," she pointed out drowsily.

"We'll just run our businesses from bed." He pulled the pins from her tousled hair and tossed them aside. His teasing grin disappeared. "Marry me, Keri."

She pressed her fingers against her trembling lips. "Oh, Ryan." Her voice choked up. "I was all ready for you to suggest an affair, not marriage."

"Affair?" Ryan looked pained. He settled her head in the hollow of his shoulder and pulled the sheet up over their rapidly cooling bodies. "Oh, no. I want you with me all the time, not just on nights convenient for the both of us. And when the time comes and if you're willing, I hope we'll have our own family."

Keri sniffed. "I thought I was finally over crying," she grumbled. "I can't marry you, Ryan."

He sat up with a jerk. "What do you mean you can't marry me?" he exploded.

"It wouldn't work for us," she argued, sitting up and drawing the sheet around her shoulders. "We've both had bad marriages . . ."

"So we know what to watch out for this time around," Ryan smoothly countered.

"We barely know each other," she lamely protested.

171

Ryan shot her a piercing look. "I'd say we know each other pretty well. Our lovemaking was merely the icing on the cake."

Keri continued to shake her head.

"And don't try using Lacy as part of your argument," Ryan added grimly. "The two of you are already fond of each other." He pushed her back against the pillows. "We complement each other, Keri." His hands worked their old magic on her body again. He used the tip of his tongue to tickle the corner of her lips.

"No," she moaned, but her negative answer had nothing to do with his lovemaking.

"I'll let you drive my Porsche," he cajoled.

"I don't like fast cars." She began to move sinuously under his expert touch.

"We'll go to Hawaii on our honeymoon." His hand moved lower in a circling motion.

"I hate the tropics."

Nothing more was said for a long time as they became lost in their feverish lovemaking.

"Marry me," Ryan said once more, but Keri was already asleep—or pretending to be.


"I've compromised you; you have to marry me," Ryan announced, trying a different tactic during breakfast the next morning.

"That hasn't been an issue for almost eighty years." Keri calmly spread raspberry jam on her toast.


"Marriage to me means you'll always have someone to scrub your back for you," Ryan pointed out during their shower after breakfast.

"I have a long-handled brush." She ducked so that the shower spray hit him in the face.

"I'm a decent cook and am willing to share kitchen duties," Ryan added after their lunch of wine and cheese.

"I keep plenty of frozen TV dinners on hand."

"You said that you love me," Ryan said, resorting to emotional tactics that evening as they lay in bed.

"I do." Keri turned her head to kiss his throat. "I'm just afraid that marriage would spoil our love. What we have here is unique. I don't want it ruined."

"You can't ruin what we have," Ryan stated, picking up their argument the following morning.

"You can if that love hasn't had time to take root in order to survive. We have plenty of time to find out."

"I don't want plenty of time. I want to marry you now."

"Tell you what." Ryan looked up from his lunch. "I'll even give up golf on the weekends." His expression implied that he was making the supreme sacrifice.

Keri didn't see it that way. "You don't play golf."

"I'm not going to give up asking you, Keri," Ryan persisted late that night in bed. They lay with their bodies pleasantly curved against each other, sated from their lovemaking.

"No more, Ryan!" she almost snapped. "I told you that even though I love you, I won't marry you. I don't want to hear about it anymore!"

## CHAPTER ELEVEN

Keri balanced a bag of groceries on her hip, unlocked the back door, and pushed it open with her hand, which held several hangers of dry cleaning. She cursed softly when the bag threatened to tip over before she finally set it on the kitchen counter.

"Oh, no!" she moaned while unpacking the food. The can of grapefruit juice had been placed on top of the loaf of bread, and during transport, two eggs had broken in the carton. She rained a string of curses on the box boy who had packed the bag.

"Bloodthirsty as always." Two arms slid around her from behind, and a pair of lips nuzzled her neck.

*"You!"* Keri spun around and glared at Ryan. " 'Take the Porsche, Keri,' " she mocked, waving her forefinger at him. "I barely made it to the gas station on the corner!"

Ryan shrugged and flashed her a loving smile and attempted to placate her. "Now, honey . . ."

"Don't call me honey." She enunciated each word with deadly precision.

Ryan could see that Keri wasn't to be mollified easily. He grinned. Even after almost six months of marriage, she still refused to let him have his way all the time.

"When I used to call you honey, it was part of an effort

174

to get you into my bed. Now that you're there . . ." He lifted his shoulders.

"I don't want you to put me in a good mood." Keri was trying very hard not to smile. "It's been a bad day, beginning with a car running on fumes, and ending with half the groceries ruined one way or another. I'd like to remember all of this for a while."

"Hmm. Are you sure?" His tongue sought out the sensitive skin behind her ear. "I'd be more than willing to improve your mood for you."

Keri's knees threatened to buckle. "That's it: Blithely assume that everything can be solved with sex," she finally managed to mumble.

"Let me make it up to you about the car." Ryan's fingers found the zipper in the back of her dress and slowly lowered it.

Keri's reply was garbled when Ryan's mouth covered hers and thrust his tongue inside. He backed her against the counter until their hips cradled each other.

"Do you realize how many hours it's been since I made love to you?" he inquired.

"Twelve hours, forty-two minutes, and fifteen seconds, but who's counting?" Keri nuzzled his throat, inhaling the warm, musky scent of his skin. Her hand passed over the bulging front of Ryan's slacks. "Obviously you've forgotten to tell your body that it wasn't all that long ago."

"You're seducing me, wife," he accused in a low voice, digging his fingertips into her buttocks.

"I haven't had enough time to do that," she protested with a suggestive smile.

"And here I thought Christmas wasn't until next week." Ryan used his teeth to pull the neckline of Keri's

175

dress down. "I think I should unwrap this gift now instead of waiting."

"Ryan, we found out the last time that the kitchen isn't the most comfortable place for making love." Even as Keri protested, she was busy pulling his shirt free of his slacks.

"I'm not sure I can make it upstairs." His fingers teased the elastic band of her bikini pants.

"Darling, you can *make it* just about anywhere," she quipped.

"Okay, that does it." Ryan lifted Keri up and slung her over his shoulder.

"Ryan!" Keri screeched, only to be silenced by a loving pat on her rear.

"Just be patient, my love." He climbed the stairs amidst Keri's complaints that she felt like a sack of potatoes. "You sure don't feel like one," he said, leering, setting her down on the bed and hastily stripping off her dress, slip, and pantyhose; then he worked on his own clothing.

"I didn't put the milk away," Keri said, running her hands lovingly over Ryan's now naked body.

"Doesn't matter. The carton was leaking anyway." He was occupied with her panties.

*"Leaking?"* Her cry of dismay was abruptly cut off by Ryan's probing fingers in the warm center of her femininity. "It just hasn't been my day," she moaned.

"Then I'll just have to make up for it, won't I?" Ryan continued to taste and savor Keri's lips. Her throat arched up and purrs of delight sounded in the otherwise silent room.

Keri, in turn, stroked, teased, and fondled Ryan into mind-bending pleasure. She always delighted in the freedom she had to explore his body. Not a day went by in which she didn't marvel that this sensual and exciting man was all hers. And not a day went by that she didn't thank the Fates for the fact that Ryan had not listened to her constant rejections of his marriage proposals.

For the entire week after they had first made love, Ryan had landed on Keri's doorstep each morning for breakfast with a bag of Bavarian-cream–filled doughnuts in hand. He would make his first proposal of the day, stating that marriage to him would also mean rich cream-filled doughnuts every morning for breakfast. He took her to lunch each day and proposed; then he sent flowers to her office with beautifully written proposals; and he proposed to her again over dinner every evening. Each night ended with a soul-destroying kiss and the reminder that there would be so much more if she'd marry him.

He didn't try to make love to her again. Keri lasted ten days, and there were times when she wondered how she had lasted *that* long! When she finally accepted his proposal, he wasted no time in bundling her into his company jet and flying to Nevada.

Keri's deepest fear had been that marriage would turn Ryan into another Don and that he would want her to turn into the perfect little housewife. Ryan quickly proved her wrong on that point.

Ryan was proud of Keri's professional accomplishments and thought nothing of letting people know it. It was with his encouragement that she opened her second office on the other side of the city. She offered the management position to Barb first, and when Barb turned it down, Keri offered it to Cassie, who eagerly accepted it.

And Ryan kept all his promises. He took Keri to Hawaii for their honeymoon; he helped with meal preparations and the cleaning up; he was always available as a back-scrubber; and one of his wedding gifts to Keri was a gold-plated key to the Porsche. He didn't even watch the golf matches on the TV.

Lacy was thrilled to have Keri for a stepmother and knew she had an ally when boys showed up for dates. Ryan was an overly protective father, and Keri delighted in teasing him about it.

"Heaven help one of those boys if they lay a hand on your daughter, even though I've noticed that your hands aren't entirely innocent when it comes to *my* body," she gibed.

"It's different for us: We're married," he argued mildly.

"I'm talking about before we were married."

"Lack of control, then." Ryan proved the truth of his statement by teasing the top of her thigh.

Keri was happy in her marriage to Ryan. She was glad to know that when she woke up each morning, Ryan's body was curled protectively around her.

It had been a busy and surprising day for Keri. She finished the last of her Christmas shopping after work and headed for home.

Since Ryan had already called to say he'd be late, she still had plenty of time to prepare a casserole for dinner. She also took the time to change into a jade-green soft velour caftan edged with gold braid. Her hair had been pulled back and held with two tortoiseshell combs. She poured herself a glass of wine and carried it into the living room. Then she sat in a chair, watching the brightly twinkling lights on the Christmas tree. How much fun they had had decorating it! Lacy would be spending Christmas Eve with them, and Ryan and Keri would have dinner on Christmas Day with Amanda and Cal.

Keri was still lost in her thoughts when Ryan walked in the back door.

"Whew, what a day," he said, pulling his tie loose and unbuttoning his collar. "Hi, baby." He leaned over to kiss her deeply. "I hate to tell you this, but I'm starved."

"Dinner will be ready soon." She flashed him a not-quite-normal smile.

Ryan's brows met together in a frown. "Is everything all right?"

"Fine." Keri stood up and gave Ryan a kiss calculated to drive thoughts of dinner out of his mind. "Now are you satisfied?"

He slowly shook his head. "Far from it, but I'm sure we can take care of it if you care to go upstairs."

"For a man who turned thirty-seven last month, you certainly have a lusty appetite," Keri teased. Hearing the timer go off, she headed for the kitchen.

Ryan picked up Keri's wineglass and sipped the chilled Chablis while following her into the kitchen. "I talked to Lacy today. I told her I'd pick her up around one. Do you want to go with me?"

Keri hesitated. Her previous meetings with Ryan's ex-wife hadn't been auspicious. Stella had disliked Keri on sight and openly voiced her malicious opinions to both Lacy and Ryan. Father and daughter ignored her vicious remarks, and Ryan let Stella know in no uncertain terms that he didn't appreciate her taunts.

Keri barely touched her dinner that evening and was unusually quiet during the meal. Ryan kept casting her worried glances.

"Are you sure you're feeling okay?" he asked her again as Keri washed the dinner dishes and he dried them.

"The stores were just so hectic," she explained, but she didn't look at him as she replied. "I picked up a cute blouse for Lacy."

After the dishes were finished and put away, they returned to the living room. Keri walked over to the tree and picked up a gaily wrapped package.

"I bought something for you today." She held out the slim, flat package.

"Oh, you mean all those other packages marked with my name aren't for me?" Ryan joked, taking the package from her.

"I may let you have them." Keri smiled faintly, sinking down onto the couch.

Ryan glanced at Keri briefly before he tore the wrapping off the package. It turned out to be a book.

*"A Father's Handbook?"* He chuckled, turning the book over in his hands. "Is this supposed to help me get through these experimental years of Lacy's?"

"Open it," Keri quietly advised.

Ryan opened the book and studied the whimsical cartoon. He became very still.

"When did you find out?" His voice came out a little strained.

"Today. I took an early lunch and went in to see Joyce. I had taken one of those at-home tests a couple days ago and it came out positive."

Ryan looked up at Keri's face, which appeared pale.

"What did she say? Are you all right?" He could feel his insides twisting up.

Keri nodded. She blinked rapidly to keep back the

180

tears. "You're going to be a father; can't you say any more?"

Ryan pulled her into his arms and held her tightly. "Oh, God, Keri," he groaned, already imagining the worst. "When?"

She laughed shortly. "That weekend you kidnaped me to Mexico. You remembered to pack a change of clothes but no protection." She hastily added, "But I'm not blaming you or anything. It was just one of those things."

Ryan did some quick figuring. "That was just before Thanksgiving."

Keri nodded.

Ryan looped a handful of Keri's hair around his fist and gently pulled her head back. "The idea of you carrying my child is beautiful, but your health is much more important to me," he stated fiercely.

"My health is a hundred percent improved from last time," she said sincerely, but her eyes couldn't hide the truth from him. She was very frightened. Keri could still remember the pain and sickness she had endured months before.

"Did you get a prescription for the nausea?" He cradled her tightly against him.

She nodded. "Ryan," she said in a small voice, "I'm frightened."

"Don't be afraid, babe. I'll always be here for you," he vowed fervently. "Sweetheart, I'm happy and I love you very much." He knew the reason for her fears because he hadn't forgotten the day of her miscarriage either. Her pleas that he not let her die had rung in his ears for weeks afterward. He had sworn never to leave her alone, and he made sure that he kept that promise. "Do you want to tell your family when we go over there?"

181

"Yes." She was so glad to have him with her.

Ryan still held Keri as he leafed through the book of cartoons. He chuckled over several. "I wonder what your strange food cravings will be," he mused, pleased to earn a genuine laugh from Keri.

That night Ryan made love to Keri slowly, using every ounce of control he had. When she was positive she would go mad from his deliberate caresses and the flicking of his tongue over her sensitized skin, he took her to realms of pleasure never revealed before. Then they slept, still lying in each other's arms.

Lacy was overjoyed when Ryan told her. "Remember all those times you used to ask for a baby brother or sister?" Ryan had said. "Well, I finally did something about your request."

Amanda was more to the point. "Do you feel all right?" she asked once she had gotten Keri alone.

"Yes," she replied, then added in a more urgent voice: "I want this child, Amanda. I want to give Ryan his son."

She raised a perfectly arched eyebrow. "You may have a girl."

Keri laughed. Trust Amanda to have a pragmatic answer. "If you can have boys, so can I!"

Christmas was beautiful. Keri loved the diamond pendant and earrings Ryan gave her, and he admired the intricately carved pen-and-pencil desk set she gave him.

"Do you still want to go to Jason's party on New Year's Eve?" Ryan asked sleepily on Christmas night.

"Of course." Keri yawned. She snuggled closer to his naked body. Part of her wanted to "persuade" Ryan to make love to her. Another part decided to wait until morning, when she would be more awake to enjoy it.

Ryan's hand slid possessively over Keri's silk-covered abdomen. He had gotten up that morning to find some soda crackers to soothe Keri's queasy stomach. He wasn't sure if morning sickness was supposed to start so early, but he had an idea that Keri's apprehension regarding her pregnancy was part of the problem. He knew he would make sure always to be there for her. She would need a lot of support in the coming months.

"I just thought of another good reason why you had to marry me," he murmured, brushing aside her hair and exploring her nape with his lips and teeth.

He could sense her smile. "Oh? And what is that?"

He nestled his body spoon-fashion against her. "No need for an electric blanket; therefore your electric bills are cut."

Keri turned in his arms. "I have a better reason."

"You sure do!"

"Now behave. The reason I married you was so that if the house was ever broken into, I could send *you* downstairs to investigate instead of going myself. So you're right: You are very handy to have around the house."

What began as touching and kissing ended in sleepy, languorous lovemaking.


Keri's pregnancy was very normal and uneventful. Her morning sickness was curbed by the pills Joyce had prescribed, and all too soon her figure altered. But her fears still remained below the surface. Would she lose this child also? The child she wanted so badly?

What didn't ease her peace of mind was Jason's suffering a heart attack and Ryan's having to handle both Arizona offices and traveling to the new offices in Houston and Dallas. He was sometimes gone almost two weeks out of each month.

"I don't want this," he told her one morning just before he left for the airport to fly to Houston.

"I know." Keri managed a bright smile. Lately she had been feeling decidedly unglamorous with her rounding figure, but she didn't want to worry Ryan more than necessary. He had enough pressure on him without her adding to it.

"Oh, love," Ryan sighed, putting his arms around her, "you're hating my trips like hell and I can't blame you. I'm just glad that Jack Collins is just about ready to take over the trips to Texas."

"I'm sorry, Ryan." She sniffed. "Damn. Get out of here before the waterworks begin again."

The nights Ryan was gone, Keri walked aimlessly through the house and rarely fell asleep before dawn.

One time Keri went to pick Ryan up at the airport and arrived early. She didn't expect to see him walk across the terminal, talking to a tall, svelte, brown-haired woman whose appearance could only be described as chic. Keri quickly masked her misery when she saw Ryan coming toward her with a broad smile on his lips.

"Mmm, you smell good." He kissed her thoroughly, his tongue darting in for the sweet taste of her mouth. "Taste good too," he murmured. His eyes looked her over with frank male appreciation mingled with husbandly lust. "I like the new hairstyle."

"Do you?" She lifted a hand self-consciously to her hair, which had been cut in a short cap of curls just that morning. "It's been so hot lately and this is much easier for me to take care of. You don't think it's too short, do you?"

"It makes you look like a pixie." He wrapped an arm around her shoulders as they walked out of the terminal.

Keri's eyes couldn't help but stray toward the woman, who was stepping into a cab.

"Lovely woman," she commented all too casually.

"Who?" Ryan unlocked the passenger door of the Audi and assisted Keri into the car.

"The woman you were talking to."

Ryan slid behind the wheel and turned to place a possessive hand on Keri's rounded abdomen.

"He's really kicking up a fuss," he murmured. "Just like his mother." He nibbled at the corner of her lips. "You're beautiful."

"I'm fat," she stated flatly.

"You're sexy."

"I resemble a Sherman tank."

"You've always had such soft skin," Ryan murmured while his lips traveled down her neck.

"I cry all the time," Keri mumbled.

"You even know how to cry sexily." He picked up her hand and laid it on his chest. "I'm yours, Keri, and you're mine. If that woman was beautiful, I didn't really notice, because the only woman who matters to me is you. All I cared about was getting home to you."

Keri flashed him a watery smile. "How have you put up with me lately?"

Ryan tapped her nose with his forefinger. "Easily: I love you."

Except Keri grew more awkward with each passing day, and the heat bothered her a great deal. She had

185

stopped working during the beginning of her eighth month, and that was when Lacy came to stay with them.

Keri was grateful for the young girl's company during the day. She helped with the finishing touches on the nursery, which had been decorated in spring green and white with Winnie-the-Pooh wallpaper.

During the evenings Ryan grumbled at the hours Lacy spent on the phone or the many boys who stopped by to see her.

"You're being the overprotective father again," Keri teased him one evening while he rubbed her back, which had been aching a great deal lately.

"Damn right. I can be an overprotective and jealous *husband* when I need to be too."

"You don't have to worry about Wilma the Whale here," she said sourly.

Ryan grasped Keri's arms and gently pulled her upright into a sitting position. "Let's get something clear here, wife," he said firmly. "All your self-pitying remarks aren't going to get you anywhere. I'd love you if you were carrying quintuplets and resembled the Empire State Building. You're exasperating at times, and you've led me on a merry chase, but I still love you and lust after your gorgeous body."

"I was so afraid!" Keri blurted out.

Ryan rubbed her cheekbone gently with his thumb. "Why were you afraid?"

She took a deep breath in order to organize her thoughts. "You've always known what you've wanted, Ryan." She ventured a small smile. "I'm a prime example of one of your goals. Yet, I was afraid of losing you."

*"I* was the one who kept proposing to *you,"* he reminded her.

Keri nodded. "Yes, but I had been married before and had thought it would last for at least fifty years. I was somewhat crushed when Don and I divorced, but it was nothing compared to what I would feel like if you and I parted. I never cared for him the way I love you, so I knew the pain would be much greater."

Ryan rained kisses over her face. He had never realized how deeply Keri felt for him until that moment. He was secure in her love for him, but this was the first time he understood the depth of that love, and it humbled him. There was so much he wanted to say, but he knew something light needed to be said before Keri broke into tears again. He nuzzled her neck with his lips and cupped her full breast with his hand.

"What size bra are you wearing now?"

Keri slapped his hand aside. "You'd better cast one of them in bronze, because in a few weeks I'm sure they'll go right back down to where they were." She winced and rubbed the small of her back. "Two more weeks," she wailed, resting her forehead against his chest, although leaning forward with her round tummy was tricky.

"I'm remaining home with you until the baby comes." He resumed kneading the ache from her spine. "That way I can be with you in case we have a baby who decides to come during the day."

"How do I deserve you?" she murmured sleepily.

"By eating your vegetables and cleaning your room." He found her nape absolutely exciting. "Would you like to take a warm bath? It may make you feel better."

Keri shook her head. "I'll never get out of the tub."

"You will if I help you."

She shook her head again. "Just hold me, Ryan. I love it when you hold me," she said with delight.

Unfortunately, Ryan was beginning to get ideas other than just holding Keri. He hadn't made love to his wife in a while, and just holding her was sheer torture.

"You weren't as afraid as you thought you were, sweetheart, or you wouldn't have taken a chance with me," he whispered in her ear. "And fifty years from now, when we're sitting in our rocking chairs, watching our grandchildren, I'll remind you of that chance and how well it paid off."

Except that Keri had fallen asleep. Ryan carefully tucked her into bed and went across the hall to his office while wondering what time Lacy would come in from her date and if she'd invite that pimply-faced football player in.

Keri woke up suddenly a few hours later. Her twinges had turned into full-fledged pains that took her breath away.

"Oh! Ryan!" she moaned, then breathed sharply when another pain hit her. *Ryan!* Her voice rose.

He was in the bedroom in a flash. One look at Keri's wild eyes told him enough. Had Lacy come home yet? he wondered. He ran back out into the hall and halfway down the stairs. The couple seated on the couch quickly parted.

"Lacy, the baby's coming. Call Joyce Reynolds and tell your boyfriend to go home," he shouted as he ran back up the stairs. "And if that pubescent lothario had his hands where I think he had them, I'll kill him!"

"Oh, Ryan," Keri groaned when he ran back into the bedroom. "Can't you ever stop acting the overbearing father? I'm about to lose three hundred pounds and

188

you're making jokes." She breathed in through her nose and reached out for his hands.

"Okay, wife, let's go get us a baby." He brought her fingertips to his lips. He assisted her to her feet and reached for the overnight case Keri had packed the week before.

"I have to get dressed," Keri protested as Ryan guided her to the door.

"You don't have time to get dressed," he argued.

"I'm not going to the hospital in my nightgown," she snapped. "Just bring me that coral cotton dress I wore several days ago."

Muttering between gritted teeth about stubborn women and how the baby could end up being born at home, Ryan tore the dress off the hanger. In a matter of seconds he had pulled Keri's nightgown over her head and exchanged it for the dress.

"Now can we go?" he demanded, exasperated.

"What about my underwear?"

Ryan cursed under his breath. "Keri, this is one time when you can go to the hospital and they're not going to care whether you're wearing any or not." He pushed her out the door.

"Dad, Joyce is on her way to the hospital," Lacy declared breathlessly as she appeared in the doorway.

"Here." Ryan handed her the suitcase. "The car keys are on my dresser. You drive."

Lacy stopped long enough to give Keri a reassuring hug and a kiss on the cheek before running out of the room. Ryan kept a supporting arm around Keri as they descended the stairs.

"Ryan"—she clutched at him—"I'm scared."

"It's natural for new mothers," he soothed, guiding her into the garage and assisting her into the car.

"You promised not to leave me."

"And I won't."

During the drive to the hospital Ryan comforted Keri's natural fears and successfully hid a few of his own. Right then all he cared about was Keri's health and well-being.

Joyce was waiting for them when they arrived.

"It's two weeks early," Keri said weakly.

"Babies make their own timetables, Keri." Joyce squeezed her hand. "Now, let's see how much you're dilated."

"Ryan comes with me," Keri insisted, holding on to her husband's hand in a viselike grip.

"Naturally." Joyce smiled at Ryan. "I doubt I could keep him out if I wanted to."

Ryan remained by Keri's side. There are times when a baby decides to be born as quickly as possible, and this was one of them. Ryan coached Keri with her breathing and held her hand. Throughout the delivery he deeply regretted the pain a woman endured to bring a new life into the world, not realizing that nature caused a unique amnesia. Only the joy would be remembered.

"Now, get ready to push," Joyce instructed.

Keri's face was flushed and damp from her exertions, but Ryan's whispered words of encouragement were all she heard until a lusty child's cry greeted them.

Lacy sat tensely in a chair, wishing she had the nerve to light a cigarette; however, she knew that if her father knew she was smoking, he would have a fit. Oh, well, it wasn't all that great, and she'd probably quit. It was bad enough that Ryan had caught Eric and her kissing on the couch.

*Poor Dad,* she thought with a flash of humor. *It's so hard for him to understand that I'm growing up.*

She looked up and saw Ryan, a broad grin on his face, stride down the hall. He held out his arms and pulled her into his embrace. "I hope you wanted a brother," he announced.

"Keri had a boy?" Lacy said excitedly, hugging him back. "How wonderful! When do I get to see him?"

"Right now." Ryan felt as if his smile were a permanent part of his body. Keri was fine, and now they had a son along with a daughter. No man could ask for more.

Keri awoke slowly from a long nap. She stirred and turned her head on the pillow. A garden dish sat on the nearby table, and a man's figure filled the small chair.

"Ryan?" Her voice and actions were drowsy.

He was instantly at her side. "Hello, love."

Keri's fingers brushed over his face. "You're crying," she mused.

"Now I understand when people talk about tears of joy." He took several deep breaths. "Thank you for our son. He's beautiful."

She nodded dreamily. "He has your color hair, and I'm sure he'll have your eyes too," she informed him. "Later on we'll probably see a miniature display of your temper."

"I don't have a temper," Ryan replied lazily, bestowing a nibbling kiss on each fingertip. "But I do have a beautiful wife, a beautiful son, and a daughter who I'm going to talk into baby-sitting for us for the next ten years or so. It will keep her out of mischief."

"Ryan"—Keri looked up at him with her love shining out of her eyes—"I'm not afraid any longer."

He groaned. "You tell me this at a time when I can't make love to my wife?" he teased her gently. "Well, then, I only have one answer."

"And what is that?" She pulled him down for a kiss to be remembered during the celibate weeks before they could consummate their love again.

It took a few moments for Ryan to catch his breath. "From now on we attend the businessmen's breakfast together. I don't want any other man to get the full impact of your charm over scrambled eggs."

"There's no problem there. I'm like you: I notice no other man but the one I love."

Ryan was right. They had the world. They needed nothing and no one else.